# Amazing
# Animals

# Amazing Animals

True Tales
and
Fantastic Facts

Vida Adamoli

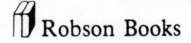 Robson Books

First published in Great Britain in 1989 by Robson Books Ltd,
Bolsover House, 5–6 Clipstone Street, London W1P 7EB

Copyright © 1989 Vida Adamoli

**British Library Cataloguing in Publication Data**
Amazing animals.
   1. Short stories in English, 1945 – Special subjects
   : Animals – Anthologies
   I. Adamoli, Vida
   823'.01'0836 [FS]

ISBN 0 86051 604 0

Printed in Great Britain by T. J. Press (Padstow) Ltd, Padstow,
Cornwall

TO MICIA
My best enemy and very own
Amazing Animal

# Introduction

When my friend Ellen was discovered lurking at the dead of night among bushes in the garden of a block of flats, she confessed to the janitor that she was not planning a break-in but simply trying to 'borrow' a tom for Parsley, housebound and on heat. Another friend waited three years, until threatened with immediate divorce, before banishing his great shaggy-coated, slobbery mongrel from the martial bed. I myself, a person not easily cowed, have allowed an irritable, demanding cat to disturb my work, my sleep, my social life and generally rule me with an iron paw.

This is not unusual; people lavish love and respect on creatures as diverse as goldfish, hedgehogs and stick insects. And social status, professional standing or intellect don't come into it. An Oxford don can be as sentimental about his dog as a taxi driver – or the Queen of England, for that matter, whose posse of spoiled corgies are served chopped liver punctually every afternoon at four.

This book is for those whose affections have been captured by animals – furry or feathered, slippery, crawly and even slimy. And also for those who haven't yet succumbed but can't resist an animal story when it appears in the press. All the animals featured are special; either exceptionally talented, intelligent, courageous, loyal or wicked. They include talking elephants, psychic cats, passionate pigs, heroic dogs, evil wolves, compassionate dolphins and a 30 ft female python who plays nursemaid to three-year-old Karin Belang. Although cats, dogs and the higher primates inevitably feature more prominently, even weird lake monsters and an agoraphobic owl with a fear of flying get a look in.

In search of material I read through hundreds of newspapers and many books. Some of the stories I found made me laugh, some made me sniffle. Others told of such altruistic bravery, kindness and nobility of spirit I felt very humbled in my flawed humanity. But whether we love them, are amused by them or simply find them fascinating, the fact is that animals have something to teach us all.

# Koko and All Ball

As one of the first gorillas taught to use sign language, Koko had no problems communicating to Dr 'Penny' Patterson her desire for a cat – she kept pulling two fingers across her cheeks to describe whiskers. Dr Patterson was not at all surprised by the request. *The Three Little Kittens* and *Puss in Boots* were among her favourite stories and cats were often mentioned during her lessons.

In June 1984 she was given a tailless male from an abandoned litter. 'Love that,' Koko signed rapturously examining the little scrap she later named All Ball. At thirteen, and of breeding age, the kitten brought out her maternal instincts. Treating Ball like a baby gorilla, she carried him tucked in her thigh and tried to make him nurse. When feeling playful, however, she dressed him in bits of material and hats or signed to him that they should tickle each other – one of her favourite games. Sometimes Ball would bite or scratch and when he did she called him 'obnoxious'. But usually she described him lovingly as 'soft good cat'.

Then in 1984 a tragedy occurred. All Ball was run over by a car and killed. Koko was grief-stricken and, refusing all comfort, went into deep mourning. A long time was to pass before she was able to accept another kitten as a substitute.

In 1903 Andrew Jackson Jr, of Munich, Tennessee, designed a pair of spectacles for chickens. His purpose was not to correct faulty vision, but to protect the birds' eyes from each other's pecking beaks. More recently, in 1959, Bertha Dlugi of Milwaukee patented a bird nappy or diaper. The minuscule triangle of fabric enabled pet birds to fly around the house without depositing unwelcome droppings.

Up until the late nineteenth century leeches were used to suck blood from the veins of patients in the belief it would draw out the 'evil vapours' causing their disease. The recent revaluation of the leech has resulted in such a flood of demands that in 1983 they were declared an endangered species and leech farms were established to protect the supply. In 1987 alone doctors at St Bartholomew's Hospital in London used 96,000 of these parasitic worms in their treatments. Now, in the era of transplants, micro surgery and many other medical miracles, they are being rescued from the ignominy of primitive medicine. Plastic surgeons say that attaching a hungry leech – which can drink two fluid ounces in 10–20 minutes – to the grafted skin helps improve bloodflow and substantially increases the chance of the graft skin taking.

# Cher Ami

Cher Ami (Dear Friend) was a homing pigeon brought to Europe by the American Expeditionary Force to serve with an infantry unit in France. He successfully delivered twelve messages while with them, the last – and most vital – on 4 October 1918.

On that day the situation of his unit in the Argonne Forest in north-east France was desperate. They had suffered severe casualties in the heavy bombardment by German artillery and, without the speedy arrival of reinforcements, risked being wiped out.

An SOS message was secured to the bird's leg and he was dispatched to the division headquarters. All the soldiers watched his departure with bated breath. But as Cher Ami soared into the air he was immediately hit by a German bullet and plummeted to the ground. Amid the general despair one lone voice rang out. 'Cher Ami,' it urged. 'Go home!'

Obeying the command, the brave pigeon flapped its wings and laboriously took flight again. But the German marksmen had him in their sights and within seconds the bird caught a second bullet in the breastbone. Miraculously he wasn't killed. As he struggled to gain height, a third bullet tore his right leg off and a fourth shot out one of his eyes.

Unbelievably Cher Ami was still alive and despite the horrific injuries struggled on to complete his mission. It took him twenty-five minutes to fly twenty-four miles through a barrage of gunfire before he collapsed in a bloody heap of feathers on the roof of the division headquarters. But the SOS message was still hanging from the ligaments of his torn-off leg, help was sent and the unit was saved.

Nobody expected the bird to survive his injuries but he did. At the end of the war Cher Ami was presented with the Croix de Guerre, one of France's highest awards for gallantry in battle. He returned to the USA in April 1919 where, less than two months later, the avian hero died.

Staff at Marwell Zoo near Winchester were convinced that their elderly Siberian tiger, Milko, was sterile. For despite being healthy and enjoying an active love life, the seventeen-year-old male had never managed to father any offspring. But nature works in mysterious ways and when in 1989 he was introduced to four-year-old Soyuz the result was a surprise set of triplets. The happy event was also embarrassing because, according to regulations controlling European zoos, Marwell was not supposed to produce any more tiger cubs until 1992. The couple were not separated, however. Instead Soyuz was given a special contraceptive implant to ensure against further amorous accidents.

When George the Mississippi alligator died at London Zoo in the mid 1950s, he was thought to be over a hundred years old. He had a reputation for attacking and even killing his companions.

Jeff Barry was in Nassau Sound, off the tip of Florida, when his boat collapsed. He was attempting to swim ashore using two floating cushions when he was suddenly confronted by hunting sharks moving in for the attack. Jeff was convinced death was just minutes away when a school of porpoises arrived on the scene and kept the sharks at bay by swimming in circles around him. The porpoises protected him for twelve terrifying hours until he was finally rescued.

In 1986 a record 11,830 dogs entered for Cruft's 90th show. Emma, an Airedale bitch, was chosen as 1986 Top Dog. Star of the show, however, was a bulldog called Cuthbert who was the Reserve Best and showed his contempt for the proceedings by eating his rosette.

The bush cricket is the fastest communicator of any animal, with less than thirty seconds between call and response. They 'hear' sounds with 'ears' in their legs.

In 1979 a Holstein cow from a dairy farm in Richmond, Indiana, set a world record by producing 55,600 lbs of milk – five times the national average. The following year she became the first cow in recorded history to produce over 100,000 lbs (11,765 gallons) of milk in two successive lactations.

Before the chimpanzees made their famous tea-party debut at London Zoo, there was a gorilla named John Daniel who visited the zoo daily with his owner to give a performance of drinking tea using a fork and spoon.

# Clever Hans

Kluge Hans – or Clever Hans as he's known in English – was a Russian stallion and Germany's most celebrated intellectual wonder horse. Owned by Wilhelm von Osten, a retired Berlin schoolmaster who discovered him in 1900, the horse soon became his most remarkable pupil, displaying a special talent for arithmetic. Using his right hoof for digits and his left for tens, Clever Hans would tap out the correct answer to elementary mathematical problems chalked up on a blackboard. He was also able to spell out simple words and phrases in German by tapping out the corresponding number to a letter – for example, three taps for C, eight for H, etc.

By 1904 he was famous and curious crowds thronged into the courtyard of the house where he lived with von Osten to watch his midday show. Scientists were totally baffled by Clever Hans's abilities and in 1907 it was decided to appoint Oskar Pfungst, a young psychologist of Berlin University, to make a study of his performances. Von Osten, who'd never made any money out of displaying the horse, was only too happy to agree.

Pfungst quickly noticed that Clever Hans was only able to respond accurately when his questioner, who was not necessarily von Osten, knew the answers. He also failed when he was blindfolded. This made it obvious that somehow or other the horse was receiving visual prompting. He discovered that the questioners were unconsciously making slight movements that were giving Clever Hans the clues he needed to come up with the correct answers. For example, after putting a question to the horse, the person would then lean forward anxiously and this was the signal for the stallion to start tapping his hoof. When he had tapped out the correct figure, the questioner would then relax, unwittingly moving his head or straightening his back. At this point Clever Hans would realize he'd satisfied his questioner and stop tapping.

Pfungst came to the conclusion that the horse had no real mathematical ability but had learned to respond to sensory clues. What he couldn't disprove, however, was that a horse who could read minimal body language with such accuracy and sensitivity fully deserved to be called 'Clever'.

Barney Hewlett lives in an Essex manor house set in 22 acres with his two-year-old pet puma, Merlin. Merlin is the perfect pet. He obediently comes when called, is completely housetrained (he uses an outsized litter tray) and purrs with pleasure when Barney takes him for a ride in the car. He's also lazy. If he gets tired when they're out exercising, he jumps on Barney's back for a piggy-back ride.

# Mad Bad Max

In August 1976 one of the most bizarre civil action cases in Texan legal history took place. A miniature six-year-old schnauzer called Max was accused of breaking and entering the house next door and raping Dollie and Sen-le, two pedigree Pekinese. According to Georgè Milton, the Pekinese's outraged owner, Max had crashed through a plate glass window in his mad excitement to get at them and make them pregnant. Mr Milton was suing for the damage to his house and the cost of the bitches' abortions.

But the Grand Prairie Judge Cameron Grey ruled there was not enough evidence to prove Max guilty and dismissed the case. Under cross-examination Mr Milton was forced to admit that, although he had identified Max in court as the guilty party, he had originally claimed the rapist to be – a poodle!

In January 1989 a white shark measuring 6.7 metres long and weighing 2 tons was captured in the Tunisian waters of Ghar el Melh. There was a long and ferocious battle before local fishermen finally landed the monster.

Michael Stead paid £2.50 for his hampster, Honey. When she escaped from her box on the way back from the pet shop, however, squeezed through the dashboard and began gnawing away at the car's heating system she cost him quite a bit more. The garage's bill for dismantling the car to find the rodent, then repairing the damage was £160.

# Honey

The congregation of a Lincolnshire church were surprised and amused when a small Tortie Burmese began turning up every Sunday and taking her place on a back pew. She would sit erect and attentive all during the long service, slipping out quietly with everyone else at the end. The cat became such a talking point that eventually the new vicar had to confess that the feline worshipper was called Honey and she was his pet.

At first Honey had seemed like a normal kitten: curious, vocal and adventurous, qualities shared by all her breed. But soon she was manifesting what could only be described as a religious vocation. She became enraptured if he played choir music, listened intently when he rehearsed his sermons and always insisted on following him to church.

The parishioners loved Honey but the presence of the pious cat in the House of God made the clergyman's superiors definitely uneasy. All attempts to keep her at home, however, failed and now Honey is a regular – and respected – member of the congregation.

The Lincolnshire cat isn't the only religious feline, however. In 1988 a tabby walked into a Buddhist temple in Kuala Lumpur, Malaysia, and joined the monks gathered in meditation. Squatting on its haunches, in the nearest it can manage to a lotus position with front paws pressed together, it has joined every midday meditation session since and the monks believe it is the reincarnation of an ancient Buddha.

G Harding of Islington, London, owns two thieving Siamese cats called Dandelion and Burdock. Although both are able to open cupboards, fridges and any packaging known to man, it is Burdock who is the true master of his art. On one memorable occasion he unzipped a leather flight bag, burrowed through tightly packed clothing, gnawed his way through three carrier bags and ate a quarter-kilo of extremely hard German sausage – all in under ten minutes.

# Karin and Si

Three-year-old Karin Belang lives with his large family on the fringe of an Indonesian jungle. Two years before he was born his elder brothers stole a baby python from her mother's nest as she crawled out of the egg. They took her home to rear as a pet and called her Si.

Although reptiles are acknowledged to be as emotionally undemonstrative as they are cold-blooded, when Karin was born the snake showed an immediate attraction for the tiny creature she could easily swallow in one gulp. For a large part of every day she lay with her huge body curled protectively around the baby's cot. Initially Karin's parents were perplexed and more than a little worried, but it soon became clear that the python's maternal instincts had been aroused and she wanted to take care of Karin like a child of her own.

It was the beginning of an extraordinary bond and the two have continued to be inseparable ever since. Si slithers next to the toddler when he wanders about in the wild terrain near his house, swims with him in the nearby lagoons and always shares his evening bath. The family never worry about Karin's safety when they are together. They know Si is fiercely protective and would kill any animal that threatened his life.

Si is now an awesome 30 ft long. She is capable of crushing to death humans and most animals and can swallow a goat whole. For one hour every day she returns to the jungle to hunt and re-establish contact with her natural habitat. But, like the responsible surrogate mother she is, Si never leaves little Karin for any longer.

Mankind's indulgence in sex for sex's sake – when chances of conception are zero – have resulted in sociobiologists labelling our species uniquely over-sexed. But now a new study of porcupines published in 1987 has revealed an animal with a libido of such extraordinary proportions he leaves us standing. Like other mammals female porcupines are only fertile at certain times but this makes no difference to their love life. Highly-sexed porcupines make love all year round with performances numbering up to ten times a night. The report suggests the key to understanding this phenomenon is monogamy. The porcupine indulges in such frequent sex to strengthen its pair bond in the same way humans are supposed to do.

In 1987 two French women, Helene Lavanant and Yvette Soltane, booked graves in an animal cemetery so that they can be buried next to their dogs when the time comes. The reason they took this step is the French law which forbids animals to be buried in human cemeteries. As Helene explained, 'My dog shares my life. I don't want us to be separated in death.'

In September 1976 a Japanese actress, Hitoko Tagawa, offered to have sex with an ape called Oliver in 'the interest of research'. Oliver, with a chromosome count of forty-seven (humans have a chromosome count of forty-six, apes forty-eight), had been hailed as the missing link between man and ape. Oliver's owner, lawyer Michael Miller, was so disgusted and outraged he started a £750,000 action against Japan's Nippon TV for initiating the publicity stunt.

# Laska and The Old Man

In 1984 a small miracle occurred when a man and dog, who'd never met before, came together in a remote spot and the dog saved the old man's life.

It all started when 81-year-old Norman Stephenson left his home in Bradford without informing his wife. Around the same time two white Samoyeds, Laska and Emma, escaped from their home six miles away when decorators left the front door open.

A couple of hours later Emma had returned but Laska was still missing and her owners called in the police to help look for her. Unknown to them, and for reasons nobody can explain, the husky-like bitch was heading for the same steep Pennine hillside where old Norman had wandered.

An ugly storm was brewing, gathering in intensity. Rain lashing the narrow path along which Norman was travelling caused him to slip and roll down the sharp incline into a ditch. When Laska found him he was semi-conscious and unable to move. Gently she draped her body over his, instinctively understanding that he needed warmth and protection from the elements. For an incredible sixteen hours her thick fur cocooned Norman and provided a shield from the worst of the storm. They were found the following morning by hikers and hours later Norman was recovering in hospital.

Afterwards the question that lingered in many minds was whether the sequence of events was just extraordinary coincidence – or had Laska had a telepathic warning of the old man's imminent danger and had gone to the hillside to save him?

The 1965 title for the Best Talking Parrot-like Bird awarded by the National Cage and Aviary Bird Show was won by a garrulous African grey parrot named Prudle. Prudle, who hung on to the title for twelve years until his retirement, not only has a staggering vocabulary of over 800 words but reputedly makes up his own sentences and, his owner claims, actually reasons.

# Gold

At 12.30 am on 14 January 1959 Alma Rosser went into labour with her second child. Having sold her house and with the new one not yet ready she was temporarily installed with her husband Alan and six-year-old son Julian in a rather primitive cottage nine miles south of Brecon in Wales. She woke her husband and they set off in the car for the Cardiff Royal Infirmary.

It was a treacherous night. The roads were covered by a foot of hard-packed icy snow and the wheels kept skidding dangerously. But although the car could only inch cautiously forward, Alma's contractions were coming faster and faster. As a qualified midwife she knew with sickening certainty that the baby was going to arrive well before they reached their destination. The only thing she could do was send her husband to phone 999 and prepare to deliver the baby herself.

It was pitch black except for a minimal light reflected by the snow. Alma, however, had the situation under control, except for a brief moment of panic when she felt the waters bulging and worried there was no one to rupture them. Fortunately a powerful contraction took care of that and she was able to ease the baby out, lay him on her leg and wrap him in the blanket she'd been lying on. At that point everyone arrived at once – the doctor, the policeman, an ambulance with lights flashing – and a short while later Alma and baby were safe in hospital.

Jonathon was a sickly baby and, due to a breast abscess, she couldn't feed him herself. To make matters worse the little scrap was too weak to suckle properly and took ages to get through 2 oz from the bottle. Twelve days later, however, they were able to return to the cottage, although Alan left the same day to start training for a new job in London. Alma found herself alone with her two sons, the family's blonde Alsatian bitch, Gold, and her seven-week-old puppies.

Although the cottage was well stocked with food, there was only enough milk formula to last until the next morning when it had been arranged a nurse would arrive with more. That night Alma fed Jonathon every three hours but at 6 am there was only enough milk left for half a feed. She dropped off to sleep again after nursing him and woke again at nine, puzzled and disorientated to find it was still pitch black.

Jumping out of bed she tried in vain first to open a window, then the front door. She climbed up a ladder into the loft where a strange light was filtering through two small dormer windows and looked out. What she saw made her heart sink and explained why it was pitch black downstairs and why she couldn't open the door or window. Stretching in all directions was a white featureless landscape with snowdrifts up to 20 ft high – in other words they were completely snowed in.

She kept Julian busy and unalarmed by giving him tasks to do and making their exercise in survival seem like an exciting game. But listening to the baby's continual distressed crying caused her extreme anxiety. With no milk left she first tried feeding him boiled water and sugar, then honey thickened with cornflour and dissolved in water. The situation became critical in the evening when he started to have diarrhoea – potentially fatal for such a young, sick baby. His crying by now was so weak he sounded like one of Gold's mewing puppies. The way Gold responded indicated she thought so too. On more than one occasion she pushed open the door to stand over the limp, exhausted baby, her swollen teats dripping milk and her dark eyes fixed on Alma pleadingly.

Alma stayed awake all that night terrified her baby was going to die. By morning she'd made a decision. First she isolated the puppies, then she took a bowl of warm soapy water and thoroughly sponged the Alsatian's whole underside. When this was done Gold, as though she knew Alma's intention, lay on her side so she could hold tiny Jonathon to her breast. Jonathon whimpered softly when he smelt the milk, nuzzled until he found the teat and started sucking hungrily. Gold's tail thumped happily and Alma knew what she'd done was right.

Every three hours she washed the dog and gave her the baby to nurse until, four days later, a bulldozer cleared a path to the house and rescuers arrived. By then, thanks to his canine wet-nurse, Jonathon's life was out of danger.

---

In November 1984 a dalmation named Toby led his owners John and Jackie White of Grimsby, Humberside, to their cat Ivan who'd gone into hiding after being hit by a car.

---

In early 1987 a venomous cobra, revered by many Hindus, made its home in the manager's office of an engineering factory near Goa. Religious leaders, who'd been immediately consulted, insisted the snake was not to be disturbed. The plant promptly closed down and daily prayers and offerings were made in the hope it would decide to leave voluntarily. It did – nearly three months later.

Personnel at Chester Zoo spent six months puzzled by crossed calls and phones ringing for no reason. Then they discovered the cause of the trouble. George, a Masai bull giraffe from Kenya, and the tallest giraffe ever held in captivity, (his head almost touched the 20 ft ceiling of the giraffe house) had become addicted to the electrical charge he got from licking the telephone wires running past his enclosure. The wires were removed to a safe distance and he died of natural causes in 1969 aged twelve.

In June 1985 Chester Zoo's orang-utan, was honoured by having a painting sold by the top art auctioneers, Sotheby's. The money went to the WWF.

Bozley was a very inquisitive kitten and in 1980 decided to explore her family's automatic loader. And that's when her ordeal started. Poor Bozley went through a programme of a warm pre-wash, spin and hot wash and was only saved when her owner investigated the strange bumping sound. Rushed to the vet, Bozley was given an injection and eight hours later was as right as rain.

In 1987 Frederick the elephant had to be pulled from a lake in a Danish nature park by rescue workers using a crane. Frederick toppled into the lake while being chased by seven amorous female elephants all wanting his virile attentions.

# Sugar

Stacy Wood was the headmaster of a school in Anderson, California, where he lived with his family and a cat called Sugar. When he retired in 1952 he and his wife moved to a small cattle farm in Gage, Oklahoma. Although the place was ideal for any animal, Sugar was so terrified of travelling that they reluctantly decided it would be kinder to leave her with a neighbour so she could stay in the area she'd grown up in.

Fourteen months later Stacy and his wife were milking cows in an outhouse when a cat suddenly appeared in a window. It paused for a moment, then leapt on Mrs Wood's shoulder and began purring like a train. The animal was identical to the pet they'd left behind, but Mr and Mrs Wood were too sensible and down-to-earth to allow themselves to believe it could really be her.

Later, back at the farm-house, they examined her properly. When they discovered a congenital hip joint deformation, they knew without a shadow of a doubt that the new arrival was indeed their Sugar. Stacy immediately picked up the phone and called the neighbour who was supposed to be looking after her. Rather shamefacedly he was told that Sugar had disappeared three weeks after the Woods left town.

This meant the cat had been travelling for over a year, had covered 2,000 or so kilometres, to track down the family she loved. How did she find them at a place she had no way of knowing even existed? A psychic 'homing device' seems the only possible explanation.

# The Dog That Drove Home

In 1984 American William Bowen's sight deteriorated to the point he had only peripheral vision, which meant he could just about discern forms but nothing more. He was declared legally blind and given a guide dog, Sir Anheuser Busch II, or Bud for short.

Two years later he went for a night on the town with his long-standing girlfriend and ended up pretty intoxicated. As she was driving him home a blazing row erupted and she stormed off leaving him alone in the car with Bud. William moved into the driving seat and Bud jumped into the front next to him. After he'd instructed him to bark once for a green light and two for a red, he started up the engine and together they set off for home. Trying to use the street lights as a guide, but unable to see the white line dividing the highway, William weaved all over the road until he was stopped by traffic police and arrested.

When he appeared in the court at Louisville, Kentucky, however, he tried to put the blame on Bud saying the dog had been the one doing the driving. And although he conceded that dogs were colour blind, he insisted that *his* dog could distinguish between the changing lights. The judge told the court it was the most amazing case he'd ever heard. 'The dog was doing its job,' he said. 'But Mr Bowen just couldn't keep the car in the lanes.'

Half way through the proceedings William shamefacedly changed his plea to guilty. He said he felt terrible for having tried to incriminate his faithful friend.

Mrs Osborne of Cottingham, north Humberside owned a very eccentric hen. Every night she used to climb to the top of a 50 ft elm tree at the bottom of the garden to go to sleep.

# Louise, Police Anti-Drug Agent

Louise is a 250 lb pig with a very remarkable snout. She can sniff out marijuana, heroin and any one of twelve kinds of explosives. Herr Werner, head of the regional police dog training centre in Hildesheim, picked her out of a litter in 1984 as just what the West German police force needed. At nine weeks old she was already displaying remarkable talent and soon routing out drugs buried at depths of up to 4 ft 6 in. Herr Franks was satisfied, Louise was satisfied and the local residents adopted her as a heroine.

Then in May 1985 Herr Franks was told that Louise was to be suspended from active duty. A pig, it had been decided, was not in keeping with the force's image. The announcement stirred up a storm of public protest. The Hildesheim dockers went on strike and refused to return to work until she was reinstated, the Green Party campaigned for a reversal of the decision and all sorts of people, including a local MP, began inundating the press with poems in her honour. Overnight Louise became a media star. She appeared on TV, had her photograph in newspapers and magazines, Die Zeit – the highbrow weekly – devoted an editorial to the issue, and she was invited onto the Hanover Opera stage to hear a Christmas rendering of the song 'Oh, Louisa'.

The West German police capitulated. In 1985 she was

officially declared a civil servant for her role as a police anti-drug agent. But in 1987 she'd had enough. Newspapers around the world announced her retirement to raise a family.

> When Howard M Chaplin's favourite black cocker spaniel, Peter, died he decided to assemble a collection of books about dogs as a memorial to him. By 1920 he had amassed more than ninety titles at his Rhode Island home and by 1937 the collection had grown to a staggering 1,993. The titles were in ten languages and included the first book published in England on dogs in 1570, *De Canibus Britannicus*. Now numbering more than 3,000 volumes, each bears a bookplate with a picture of the little cocker who inspired the collection.

# Greyfriars Bobby

On Candlemaker Row in Edinburgh is a large, red granite drinking fountain for dogs with a life-sized statue of a Skye terrier seated on a pillar in the centre. The dedication plaque reads: 'A tribute to the affectionate fidelity of Greyfriars Bobby. In 1858 this faithful dog followed the remains of his master to Greyfriars Churchyard and lingered near the spot until his death in 1872. With permission erected by Baroness Burdett-Coutts.'

Greyfriars Bobby is the most celebrated example of canine devotion in this country. He was the watch-dog and pet of a police constable named John Grey, who got him as a fun-loving and mettlesome puppy and took him back to the cramped, wretched flat he shared with his wife and grown-up son.

Every Tuesday night John Grey and Bobby patrolled the

big cattle market in readiness for the busy selling that started at dawn the next day. It was a big event attracting thousands of people and both man and dog looked forward to the excitement and activity. Bobby snuffled around the legs of the livestock and picked fights with visiting country dogs. John Grey – Auld Jock to his friends – met up with acquaintances from his native village and caught up on the news. The market packed up at midday, by which time Grey's stint of duty had finished. He and Bobby would then walk up Candlemaker Row, a steep street of huddled picturesque houses, to an eating-house near the gate of Greyfriars church. In 1856 and 1857 the landlord was a man called Ramsey whose cheerful wife helped bake pies, make soups and brew big pots of tea and coffee. Bobby enjoyed these visits every bit as much as his master. Everyone liked him and he knew he'd always get some titbit – occasionally even a mouthwatering bone from the stew pot.

Winters in Scotland are notoriously cold and wet and more often than not Auld Jock and Bobby returned from night patrol freezing and soaked to the skin. Although little Bobby suffered no ill effects, Grey developed an ugly, persistent cough that was visibly sapping his strength. The police doctor called in by his worried wife was uneasy and put him on sick leave, telling him not to think of returning to work until he felt better. But Auld Jock only got worse. Although nobody realized it he was suffering from tuberculosis, 'withering disease' as the people called it then. All through his long illness Bobby lay at his feet gazing up at him with sad watchful eyes. Every now and then, when the sun shone, he would perk up sufficiently to take his dog for a short walk which got everyone hoping. But on 8 February 1858 Auld Jock died and two days later was buried in Greyfriars cemetery. The mourners following the simple coffin were trailed by a small, distraught presence – Bobby.

When the ceremony was over Bobby didn't want to leave and Auld Jock's son had to pick him up and carry him struggling back to the pitiful flat where a funeral tea was waiting. Normally as greedy as they come, Bobby refused

Bill and Pauline Herbdige's tiny pond in the back-garden of their Southampton home is well stocked with lively fish. They are all, without exception, courtesy of the family kitten, Dinky. There have been no complaints from neighbours and it is a complete mystery where he gets them from. All they know is that he regularly appears with a fish flopping about in his jaws and deposits it in the water.

In 1987 Oliver Watters and his brother Ian, farmers from Llanddewi, Wales, had the novel idea of training two large wild pigs to round up their sheep. The pigs have proved so excellent at the job that the brothers now plan to train their offspring and enter them in sheep dog trials!

Six-year-old Andy the poodle, chosen from among dozens of other dogs for the canine part in the London production of the hit musical *42nd Street*, is a real star. His contract stipulates a supply of dog biscuits in his dressing room and first class travel between his home in Brighton and Victoria. In London he eats at Flounders restaurant where he's served a selection of cheeses at his regular table.

Police rushed round to the Reading home of a mortgage broker after tracing an emergency call from someone 'panting and gasping' but unable to speak. To their amused surprise they found that the 'distressed' caller was a ten-week-old Boxer puppy aptly named Mad Max. Bored at being left on his own for a whole evening, Mad Max started playing with the telephone and punched out 999.

any of the food offered to him, instead setting up a persistent, mournful howl. The noise was so unnerving that eventually Mrs Grey opened the door and let him out.

Bobby streaked down the stairs, across the court and away up the narrow street to the cemetery. Although it was locked to keep out dogs and children, the determined terrier forced an entry and found his way back to Auld Jock's half-filled grave. Once there, he lay on the boards covering the hole and went to sleep.

He was discovered early the next morning by the gardener, James Brown. The man immediately tried to chase him away, hitting out at him with his shovel and receiving threatening growls, snarls and snaps in return. It was the timely arrival of a young gravedigger that avoided the situation becoming really nasty. 'That's Auld Jock's dog,' he told him. 'He was at his funeral yesterday'. The gardener was immediately sorry for his treatment of Bobby and, to make amends, went off to get him a bite of breakfast.

And so Greyfriars Bobby's long vigil began. James Brown, who was to grow very fond of him, brought food and water to the den the dog had made under a half-toppled gravestone. Even the night policemen gave him a pat and scraps of their food when they knew who he was. And every lunchtime Bobby turned up at Mr Ramsey's eating-house always to be rewarded with some little treat, a tradition continued by all subsequent landlords. He later made friends with a soldier called Scott who taught him to understand that the sound of the one o'clock gun meant lunchtime. After that people gathered daily to watch Bobby trotting off to the eating-house when the gun fired.

On 29 March 1867 a new licensing law for dogs was passed and it was the chief magistrate at the City Chamber who paid for Bobby's out of his own pocket. He even had a collar made for him engraved with the words: 'Greyfriars Bobby from the Lord Provost, licensed'.

As the years passed Bobby's fame grew. He was painted and sketched, sometimes by well-known artists, photographed and written about. Visitors from all over the world came to gaze moist-eyed at the little Skye terrier lying on his poor master's simple grave.

On 14 January 1872, by then old and feeble, Greyfriars Bobby died. For fourteen long years he had endured countless hardships and every sort of weather for the love of a master he never forgot and refused to be separated from. A special exception was made to allow Bobby to be buried next to Auld Jock. American friends raised the money for the engraved headstone that to this day marks the spot.

Vincent Sazio of Thornton Heath, Surrey, decided one morning to give his 4 ft pet python, Monty, a live mouse as a special treat. When he returned that evening, however, he had a shock in store. The tiny 6 in long creature had not only killed the snake – it had taken a good gnaw at it too.

# Jack, The Signalman Baboon

The railroad employee manning the signal near Vitenhage, South Africa, gave passengers on that route feelings of definite unease. For carefully checking that the correct signal was up was not a man – but a chacma baboon called Jack.

Jack's position of responsibility came about when his owner, James Edwin Wide, lost both legs in a railway accident and handed his job over to his pet. The clever animal quickly learned to operate the correct levers and fetch the key to the coal bin according to the number of whistles emitted by the approaching train. At home he was equally indispensable. He pumped water from the well, weeded and tended the flowers in Wide's garden, and pushed him to work every morning in a trolley.

Delighted by the baboon's handling of the job, the railway company put him officially on the payrole. Jack's wage was twenty cents a day and half a bottle of beer on Saturdays.

He died in 1980 after nine accident-free years on the job. He was buried next to his signal box.

---

The one-humped camel is called by the Arabs 'Allah's greatest gift to mankind'.

---

# Nick The Labrador And The Stray Collie Bitch

In 1983 Nick the Labrador was out on one of his solitary walks when he met a stray collie bitch dragging a badly injured back leg. The immediate rapport they experienced can only be described as love at first sight.

Although he'd always been a loyal and reliable dog, this time Nick did not return to his owners' comfortable home. Instead the pair set off together for the London suburb of Mill Hill and made a lair beneath the bushy hedge of a neat front garden.

For two days Nick stood guard over the collie who was now unable to walk and lay licking her wound. They were noticed by the woman of the house who, touched by their plight, began putting out food for them. Despite being ravenously hungry Nick would first carry pieces of food to his companion before settling down to eat himself. The two dogs attracted the curiosity of local residents who were able to lead police to the spot after Nick's owners had reported him missing. Several people were around to witness the painful scene as he was forcibly separated from his mate and dragged howling into the van.

During the next few days Nick pined incessantly, indifferent to food or any of his usual diversions. At the first opportunity he escaped again and rejoined the collie in their lair under the hedge. This time, however, the police knew just where to find him. Nick's owners responded by being extra vigilant. He was never allowed out unaccompanied and during walks was kept securely on the lead.

Eventually, however, Nick saw a chance and seized it, streaking through the streets to the hedge in Mill Hill. But he arrived to find the wounded collie had been taken away and destroyed. Nick's plaintive howls echoed through the sedate suburban air. His owners, the police, the local residents, were all deeply moved by his grief. But their understanding and compassion came too late.

The most dangerous bird that ever existed was the Titanus, extinct during the Ice Ages. It stood at some 12 ft, had gigantic talons, a lethal hooked beak, was too heavy to fly and looked like a monstrous ostrich. Titanus could run faster than a horse and devour any animal it managed to catch – even preying on the Glyptodons, armadillo-like animals who had no other natural enemies. A 3 ft tall, long-necked bird called a Cariama is its only known living decendant. It lives in the forests of Paraguay and is also a spectacular runner, clocking up speeds of up to 25 mph.

Two African elephants nuzzling playfully.
*Oxford Scientific Films – Anthony Bannister*

Two kittens play with a baby squirrel.
*Oxford Scientific Films*

Time for a rest.
*Oxford Scientific Films – John Paling*

For two weeks every November, Christmas Island is invaded by 120 million landbased crabs. They swarm over everything: roads, tennis courts, railway lines, houses and even manage to climb walls and wire fences. During the crab takeover, most people leave their cars at home because a large crab's claws are sharp enough to puncture any tyre. Most of the year they live quietly in holes, but they can only reproduce by returning to the sea. One of the most extraordinary and breathtaking sights is the surging tide of crabs pouring over the cliffs and sweeping like great red waterfalls into the sea below.

# White Death

Twelve-year-old Newton Leslie was very excited when he set off with his father Weston, and one of his father's friends for a tuna fishing trip off the coast of Naalehu, Hawaii. For several hours all was wonderful then, shortly after the sun had set, they suddenly found themselves plunged into a real-life *Jaws* nightmare.

Newton's father had just hooked a tuna when a 19 ft long giant Great White shark weighing more than 1,000 lbs attacked their small boat. First it devoured the tuna fish, then turned its homicidal fury on the craft. With a terrifying sound of splintering wood the shark sunk its razor sharp teeth into the hull, then hit the motor and drain plug areas. It was gnawing on anything it could get hold of. Within minutes the vessel had filled with water and capsized, throwing the two men and the boy into the churning water. It was the beginning of a horrifying twelve-hour ordeal.

Fortunately Newton's father had managed to grab a 'bang stick' – a makeshift underwater gun used by divers – before their boat capsized. As the Great White lunged at him, he managed to shoot it through the head and kill it instantly. That was when the shark pack moved in, circling and shadowing them as they swam the nine miles to the nearest island.

It was a constant battle all through the night. The sharks never left them and they had to scream under the water and continually pound the surface with their hands to keep them at bay.

It was 10 am the following morning when, exhausted and suffering from shock, they dragged themselves ashore. Miraculously, however, they'd not only survived but had done so without suffering any real injury.

> The Bulldog club, founded in 1875, is the oldest specialist dog society in the world. Bulldogs are Britain's national dog emblem. The breed was derived from the earlier mastiff and was used in bull and bear baiting. One of London's once many bull arenas and bear-pits was the Bankside Bear Garden at Southwark.

# Venus

Venus was only a very tiny brown and white Jack Russell terrier, but her small body hid the heart of a lion. And she demonstrated it dramatically when her 84-year-old mistress was attacked by an enraged Friesian bull.

It happened in 1972 when Madge Comerford and Venus were taking a walk through a picturesque Sussex field. Venus was nosing around some distance away when the massive beast, who Madge probably mistook for a cow, suddenly charged. It thundered over, knocked the frail old lady to the ground and started butting her with its horns.

Alerted by her mistress's terrified screams, Venus streaked across the field to the rescue. She leapt up, sunk her sharp teeth into the bull's nose and hung on until it staggered back bellowing with pain. Once the bull had backed off, Venus shot behind it snapping at its heels until she'd managed to herd it into an adjacent field. It was an heroic, David and Goliath confrontation and – once again – David won.

During all this, Madge was able to get up and hobble to safety. Thanks to Venus she escaped with just a fractured rib and a few bruises.

Prominent political figures all accept the possibility of an attempt being made on their life. Most of them, however, expect the danger to come from something on two legs. Jimmy Carter anticipated no trouble when he took a break from the cares of the White House to go on a fishing trip in his home State of Georgia. But trouble there was – in the guise of a crazed rabbit who, teeth bared, streaked across the small lake and ferociously attacked his canoe. The intrepid President beat off his assailant with a paddle.

# Jane Goodall and David Greybeard

In 1989 Jane Goodall had studied chimpanzees in the Gombe Stream Chimpanzee Reserve in Tanzania for twenty-nine years, making it the longest field study of any community of wild animals. Her devotion to them was such that when, after seven years, her first husband decided he'd had enough, she opted to stay on alone.

She started her project at the age of twenty-three with no academic qualifications, just a deep love of animals. When

Quincey the white cockatoo was a star turn in the kiddies corner of a zoo at Flamingoland in North Yorkshire. His act included such feats as roller skating, riding a mini-bike, driving a model car and playing the piano. Adored by the children, fussed over by his trainer, Quincey fell into disgrace when, at the end of a performance, he suddenly squawked loudly: 'F . . . off!' Quincey was punished for his unacceptable language by being dropped from the show and confined to his cage.

In February 1989 76-year-old Beatrice Crabb and her white poodle, Sandy, were found dead in a shallow pond in the picturesque village of Montacute in Somerset. Although there were no witnesses, careful investigation led the police to believe that the perpetrators of the horrible crime were a pair of swans, Arthur and Leda. The graceful, aristocratic creatures first attacked Sandy when he barked at them, then turned their ferocity on Mrs Crabb when she went to her pet's rescue.

In 1987 thieves stole a mynah bird called Tommy and a rare African parrot from a pet shop in Bristol. Thirty-six hours later, however, they dumped the mynah back on the shop doorstep. Tommy's owner wasn't surprised. 'He never stops talking,' she said, 'and he swears like a trooper. They were probably scared he'd get them arrested by telling people he was stolen.' Tommy is exceptionally clever and observant. When his owner quizzed him about the robbery he was able to give her several clues.

Stefano Morini who lives near Bologna, Italy, spent ten years developing the world's smallest pig. The 'mini maialino', as he calls them, weigh a mere 20 lb when fully grown and are easily house-trained. They are also very pretty to look at.

she was two she slept with earth-worms under her pillow, and at four squatted for five hours in a henhouse to discover how chickens laid their eggs.

The first animal to accept her presence in the Reserve was a powerful male she named David Greybeard. Not only did he tolerate her following him, he actually waited for her to catch up before moving on. She was allowed to watch him eating and was fascinated to observe him stripping leaves off a twig to stick into termite holes. In her book *In the Shadow of Man*, she describes a key moment in their relationship when she offered him a ripe pine nut: 'When I moved my hand closer he looked at it, and then at me, and then at the fruit, and at the same time held my hand firmly with his own. As I sat motionless he released my hand, looked down at the nut and dropped it to the ground. At that moment, there was no need of any scientific knowledge to understand his communication of reassurance ... the barrier of untold centuries which has grown up during the separation of evolution of man and chimpanzee, was, for those few seconds, broken.' In order to gain their trust, Jane was always careful to approach the apes in a submissive and unobtrusive manner. Eventually the presence of the strange pale female primate became so familiar they would even make love while she was there. Like Dian Fossey and Birute Galdikas, who also conducted long field studies with apes, Jane discovered how much of human behaviour is rooted in that of apes. The babies also learn life skills from their mothers, apes instigate and settle quarrels, they enjoy playing and making jokes, help each other in times of crisis and go into mourning for their dead.

She learnt to recognize their distinct personalities and individual ways of interacting. There was Old Flo with the bulbous nose, a model mother who raised her offspring with gentleness and endless patience. And Mike, an enterprising young male who discovered that by banging empty kerosene cans he could cow rival males into submission.

Jane spends only four months at Gombe now, the rest of the year occupied with lecturing and lobbying on conservation issues. The bond she forged with David Greybeard, however, was the foundation stone of all her subsequent work and the time she still manages to spend with the apes is where she continues to get all her inspiration.

> Scientists have discovered a new species of whale, only 14–24 ft long, in Peruvian waters. They have called it Mesoplodon Peruvianus.

# Lassie

Lassie is probably the most famous dog in the whole world. Since the first movie *Lassie Come Home* hit the screens in 1943, subsequent movies and TV series have netted well in excess of £2 million. The TV series, which was syndicated world-wide, was first seen in Britain on ITV in 1956. Over the years it has won sixty-nine awards, including an Emmy for the best-ever children's programme – and there was even an American radio series with Lassie barking her 'lines'. Several international stars have reason to be grateful to Lassie too. Elizabeth Taylor, Roddy McDowel and *Remington Steele* star, Stephanie Zimbalist, all had their careers boosted by appearing in *Lassie* movies.

The original Lassie was a collie called Pal. He was bought for just $10 and soon afterwards was taken to Rudd Weatherwax's Californian kennels to be cured of his habit of chasing cars. His owner must have thought he was more trouble than he was worth, however, because he never returned to collect him. In similar situations Weatherwax had sold the animal to recuperate his fee, but he'd grown fond of the dog and decided to keep him. Pal was intelligent, willing, and quickly learned the many stunts Weatherwax taught him. He learned them so well, in fact, that when he was picked to understudy MGM's original choice for *Lassie Come Home*, he proved so clever he stole his canine rival's part. The movie made a huge impact and placed Pal's paw firmly on the ladder of success.

Weatherwax's wife, however, resented the time and attention her husband lavished on the dog. During their highly publicized divorce case, she accused him of loving Pal more than he loved her.

Pal died at the ripe old age of nineteen. Knowing that millions of children believed Lassie to be immortal, Weatherwax decided against a grave and had his ashes scattered at sea instead.

Despite the fact Lassie is supposed to be female, all the six subsequent stars have been big glossy males with the distinctive white flash on the forehead. Each dog has been taught to untie knots, unlatch doors, jump fences, swim rivers, fight off villains and affectionately lick friendly hands. In 1984 the reigning Lassie was Pal's great, great, great grandson.

Together with five other collies 76-year-old Weatherwax was training, he lived in a fortress-like ranch protected from would-be dog-nappers by an enormous spiked iron fence and several armed bodyguards. The collies' life-style was suitably privileged. They were shampooed and groomed daily by skilful staff, fed on ground chicken, beef, rice and dog biscuits mixed with chicken broth – and all of them slept with Weatherwax in his specially designed giant bed.

Winston is one of America's top drug-sniffing dogs and is so successful at his job that the US underworld have found their operations seriously disrupted. In an effort to regain the upper hand, Colombian heroin dealers have put a massive £750,000 bounty on the Labrador's head.

Lord Bryron's dog was buried in the garden of Newstead Abbey. His epitaph, written by Hobhouse, runs as follows:

Near this spot are deposited the remains of one who possessed Beauty without Vanity, Strength without Insolence, Courage without Ferocity, and all the Virtues of Man without his Vices. This praise, which would be unmeaning Flattery, if inscribed over human ashes, is but a just Tribute to the Memory of BOATSWAIN, a Dog

# Passionate Bill

In 1987 Billy the boar and Sally the sow were herded into a van for what was to be a one-way trip to the slaughter house. But Billy was a very passionate porker and even the proximity of death couldn't cool his ardour. In the midst of rush hour traffic in Barnsley, Yorks, the van suddenly started lurching dangerously from side to side. PC Dave Lawrence spotted the driver fighting to keep the vehicle under control and flagged him down. He took one look in the back, realized what was going on, and called the RSPCA.

The result was trouble for the driver but a reprieve for the amorous pair. Billy and Sally were allowed to continue their honeymoon back at the farm.

When Daisy, a Friesian cow, was sold at an auction at Okehampton in Devon, she was parted from her baby calf. The separation made her so unhappy that she jumped a gate and travelled six miles across country until she found it again. Amazed and touched by her display of maternal devotion, Daisy's new owner bought the calf too.

# Bob and Percy

Very few people in the world have the privilege of forming a real bond with a wild creature of another species. These rare relationships develop slowly and are nurtured with patience, sensitivity and, above all, respect. Bob Holborn is one of those few.

It happened in Cornwall off the coast of Portreath. Bob was out in his inflatable dinghy when he noticed a lone dolphin swimming nearby. Every time he went out after that the dolphin appeared, although it always kept a cautious distance. Then Bob hit on the idea of towing rubber tubes to capture his interest, gradually shortening the ropes securing them until he'd lured him close. After about two years of these tentative overtures Percy, as he'd named him, began nudging the boat with his beak and on one memorable occasion actually lingered long enough for Bob to stroke him.

In all seasons and whatever the weather conditions, Bob never failed to turn up for their appointment. Percy always greeted his arrival with great leaps of joy but if Bob tried to get into the water with him he'd streak away. On the occasions Bob went scuba diving the dolphin would lurk around observing him from about ten yards away.

One day Bob decided he had to break the impasse and

determined to stay in the water until Percy accepted him. This was the big break-through. He lay in the water for four hours with the dolphin swimming in ever decreasing circles around him. At last the moment came when they were close enough to touch. Bob held his breath as Percy shyly felt Bob's body gently with his beak and gave him little probing pats. When he'd satisfied his curiosity, he rested his huge head on Bob's chest and let him stroke it. It was a wonderful magic moment that lasted fifteen long minutes. When it was over the two friends went for a long swim together. Bob had never believed in telepathy and yet he developed a sixth sense where Percy was concerned, always sensing exactly where in the sea he would find him.

One day Percy suddenly twisted his neck and nodded downward, indicating he wanted Bob to dive with him. This gave Bob the idea of teaching him signs and he began the lessons underwater, where Percy seemed to prefer to relate to him. He started with simple gestures: signalling left with his hand and turning left, signalling right and turning right, signs for stop, reverse, etc. Percy responded by teaching him signals too. A succession of quick nods meant approval, two nods and a biff of his beak meant the opposite! Bob used the exact same signals to express his own disapproval – like, for example, when he was investigating something on the sea bed and Percy would push him out of the way.

He also taught the dolphin to count, initially by taking off a flipper and holding up one finger, then progressing to the use of stones. Percy showed he understood by opening his mouth equivalent to the number of stones Bob laid out. If Bob tried to trick him by laying down three stones, say, and holding up only two fingers Percy would correct him by opening his mouth three times.

The dolphin's sense of humour was also a constant source of delight. One of Percy's favourite games was balancing the boat's anchor on his head then dropping it into Bob's hands – or just that little bit short! Then he would open his mouth in what looked exactly like laughter.

The medical profession first recognized the valuable healing abilities of cats in the 1970s. Since then they have played an increasingly important role in drug and alcohol addiction and are used in therapy in old people's homes and schools for the mentally handicapped. Their beneficial soothing effect has been proved with such diverse afflictions as brain damage, mental illness and heart disease.

In January 1989 Leeds Castle in Kent staged a three-day angling challenge allowing fishermen to cast their lines in its historic moat. The aim was to discover the exact dimensions of the great pike with deadly teeth who lurk in the deceptively calm waters. It was discovered that these predators, who can live as long as a man, grow to more than 7 ft and reach weights up to 34 lb. They have also begun to eat the Castle's prized black swans.

Giant pandas spend fourteen hours a day eating bamboo. This high fibre diet means that they have to defecate forty-eight times a day.

The hummingbird is the smallest bird in the world. The unique construction of its wings, which clock up seventy-eight beats a second and can move in many directions and not just up and down, allow it to hover up, down, backward, forward and even upside down. It can also accelerate to full speed at take-off and stop abruptly at its destination. The only other flying object that comes anywhere near to matching the hummingbird's flexibility is the helicopter.

The bee's eye is made up of about 9,000 facets or lenses. They each take in a minute fraction of the whole field of view and transmit it via the bee's nervous system to its brain, which then reassembles all the thousands of parts into the complete picture.

On one occasion he played with the lines joining the lobster pots to the surface and left them in a seemingly impossible tangle. But when Bob dived down to sort out the mess, Percy indicated with his head exactly which lines to twist and showed in reverse order how he'd tangled them in the first place. The job which Bob expected to last hours was done in fifteen minutes.

There were times, however, when Percy behaved very strangely. Once he began circling the boat very fast and refused to let Bob get into the sea. The second time Bob tried he took his hand in a vice grip and forced him back in the boat. Hurt, and more than a little puzzled, Bob sailed a couple of miles further on and dived into the sea there. Percy arrived immediately, laying his head on Bob's shoulder as though apologizing for his previous behaviour. Later Bob reasoned that there must have been a shark in the vicinity or some other form of danger.

Bob valued Percy as a powerful and free creature with a complex mind of his own and their friendship was one between equals. 'He's such a beautiful character,' he said in an interview given to a famous women's magazine. 'I've offered him fish but he's never taken them from me. He's given me so much but always in the name of friendship, never for gain. Percy can't ever be bought.'

---

Touring Asia while making her *Far Eastern Cooking* series, Madhur Jaffrey reported being served some very unusual meals. She ate deep-fried crickets and wasps in Thailand and a soup made of cobra, fruit bat, deer, hedgehog, bamboo rat, scaly anteater and gecko (a small lizard which tastes like chicken) in Vietnam. Gecko is a favourite with the Vietnamese. They often serve it accompanied only by a liqueur glass of its blood mixed with rice wine. They say it's excellent for hypertension.

# Hugh and Pigeon No 167

In 1940 a boy by the name of Hugh Brady found a wounded pigeon in the garden of his home in West Virginia. He nursed him back to health, ringed him with an identity tag no 167, and kept him as a pet.

The following winter Hugh was taken suddenly ill and rushed to a hospital 200 miles away where he underwent an emergency operation. He was still recovering when, on a bitter, snowy night, he heard a persistent tapping on the window of his hospital room. He called the nurse and asked her to open it for him as he couldn't get out of bed. When she did a pigeon flew in and landed with a joyful flutter of wings on his chest. Hugh knew immediately that the visitor was his bird and a look at the number on its tag confirmed it.

Pigeons are famous for their homing instincts, but on this occasion the bird wasn't returning home — he had tracked his master down to a place he had no knowlege of and had never been to before. The only explanation for the extraordinary incident is that the bond between the two had functioned as a sort of 'telepathic beacon' or 'heart magnet'.

In December 1988 the Inqilab daily newspaper reported that at least sixty-five people had been devoured by tigers in the Sundarban forest in south-western Bangladesh during the previous four months. Most of the victims were honey collectors, fishermen, and loggers.

During the Second World War British dogs played a vital role in the defence of their country. They were used to guard vital points against airborne attacks, track down parachutists, undertake liaison work and collaborate with Red Cross workers. They were also trained to lay wires across country that was under concentrated fire, to carry ammunition, and to 'smell out' enemy positions. Dogs measuring from 1½ to 2½ ft at the shoulder and capable of carrying loads of at least half their own weight were the most suitable.

# Airedale Jack

Airedale Jack, a black and tan Battersea stray who fought in World War I, was a hero among heroes.

It was 1918, the last year of the devastating war which saw millions die in the horrific trench warfare, when Jack was sent over to France to serve as messenger and guard with the Sherwood Foresters. A massive push-on was underway and shortly after his arrival Jack's battalion fought their way through to an advance post. Almost immediately, however, they found themselves ringed in by the superior strength of the enemy. During a particularly savage fusillade all communication with headquarters four miles behind the lines was cut off.

The Foresters' situation was now desperate. Unless a message could be got through and reinforcements sent, the entire battalion was doomed. It was clear that no man could hope to get through the impenetrable barrage of fire, which left Jack as their only hope. The vital message was put in the pouch attached to his collar, he was given a quick pat on the head and urged to 'go!' Every man had a prayer in his heart as he watched Airedale Jack slip quietly away, shells and flak exploding in the air all around him.

The courageous dog had been well trained. He kept low

to the ground and took advantage of any cover however flimsy. But no training in the world could protect him from a hell such as that. When the first piece of shrapnel shattered his lower jaw he bore the pain and didn't falter. The second ripped his flesh from shoulder to haunch but still he carried on, staggering from crater to crater with a desperate determination to fulfil his mission. When his forepaw was smashed, however, he could no longer walk, but he covered the last three kilometres by dragging his terribly wounded body along the ground. With the message successfully delivered and the Sherwood Foresters saved, the dog allowed himself to die.

Airedale Jack was awarded a posthumous VC and an engraved wooden stand in the Imperial War Museum honours the memory of a true hero who saved a whole British battalion from annihilation at the hands of the enemy.

A Pennsylvanian dairy farmer, Ralf McGreggor, has discovered that a diet of chocolate improves the quality of milk produced by his cows. After feeding them finely ground KitKats and other chocolates, which provide twice the energy of corn, he noticed a marked improvement in milk production. And the cows love it!

Over fifty years ago Colonel Angus Buchanan wrote a book on the Sahara. The dedication reads:

> To Feri n'Gashi
> Only a Camel
> But steel-true and great of heart.

In April 1989 Swedish scientists planned to send eight frogs up into space to mate in an anti-gravity environment. However, they all escaped before the rocket launch and the experiment had to be postponed.

# Morris The Cat For President

When in 1986 Morris the Cat was drafted as a Democratic candidate for the presidency of the United States of America, polls showed he had the highest name-recognition and approval rating among the American public of any of the candidates so far declared. Announcing Morris's decision to seek the nomination, the feline's communications director said: 'The world is going to the dogs. America needs a President with courage, but one who won't pussyfoot around with the issues of peace – a President who when adversity arises will always land on his feet.' Eight-year-old Morris, who began life in the squalor of an animal shelter, was a star of a major cat food commercial and therefore a well-known TV star. His tendency to campaign outside at night, his ability to leap on to any obstacle in his way, was seen as a particular threat to 'lap-dog' Vice-President George Bush.

Ms Eleonor Mondale, daughter of former Vice-President Mondale, made a statement on Morris's behalf: 'Morris realizes that predjudices exist but he believes, like records, they are meant to be broken. Morris gives the examples of Harry S Truman who, in 1948, became the first haberdasher to inhabit the Oval Office, and John Kennedy who became the first Catholic President in 1962. Following in this line of firsts, Morris says he intends on being the first feline, and he's jumping into this candidacy with all four paws. He wants it to be known he has undertaken to uphold high moral standards and promises there will be no nights on the tiles.' Despite the success of such luminaries as Clint Eastwood and Ronald Reagan in politics – both from showbiz backgrounds like his own – Morris didn't manage to make it to the White House.

In May 1985 a boatman crossing the Lawas river in Borneo claimed he saw the Lawas monster, a creature with a neck as big as a 40 gallon drum, eyes like electric light bulbs and a head like a cow. Wildlife experts say the 'monster' is simply a whalelike mammal known as a dugong.

# Braken

On a bitter winter's day in 1983 Ian Elliot was felling trees on his Canadian farm when a huge pine crashed down, trapping him in the water of a shallow but viciously icy stream. His back had been broken by the impact and there was no one around except his sheepdog, Braken. Instinct told Braken that he had to keep his master warm. Whimpering his distress, he carefully lay on top of him and for three hours his thick fur kept Ian's body temperature from dropping to a critical level. It was only when his sharp ears picked up the distant sound of voices that he moved. He followed the voices for over a mile until he came upon a group of lumberjacks. The dog's urgent barking and agitated manner convinced the men something was wrong and they followed him back to where Ian lay helpless.

When he finally got to hospital, the doctors said if it hadn't been for Braken's action Ian would have died of hypothermia in a matter of hours.

A fish took revenge on Sicilian fisherman, Salvatore Monteverde, whose fishing methods were both illegal and very nasty. As he leaned over the side of his boat to drop an explosive charge to kill as many fish as he could, a large fish leapt out of the water, grabbed the explosive in its mouth and carried it under the boat. Salvatore managed to leap clear before the boat blew up and swim the two miles back to the Catania shore.

# Ant

Ant was a skewbald Welsh pit pony. For twenty-four years he worked at Blaenavon Colliery in Gwent and by the time he retired in 1966 he had clocked up an estimated 70,000 miles journeying back and forth through the underground tunnels.

Because like all pit ponies he'd never learnt to crop grass and had to be hand fed, the first man who took him in found him too expensive and tiresome to have around. For a sad moment it looked as though the pony would have to be put down. Fortunately, however, Philip Davies, an ex-miner who now owned the Three Horse Shoes, offered Ant a home in the field adjacent to his pub.

Ant arrived on 6 November 1966 and the first thing he did was take an excited gallop all the way round. It was the beginning of the pony's happy retirement years. The field was next to a bus stop and few of the waiting passengers could resist the friendly pony who leaned over the fence to see what was going on. He was stroked, fussed over and plied with sweets and apples by children from the local school.

When Mr Davies died in 1975 his daughter, Tegwyn, took over the running of the Three Horse Shoes. She didn't know anything about ponies but she immediately fell for Ant and decided that the elderly pensioner deserved some extra spoiling. From then on Ant was not only given three delicious cooked meals a day, he also had a pint of nourishing stout after each serving. After a local newspaper did a story on him he became quite a celebrity. He appeared on television and a woman in Cwmbran was inspired to write a poem about him.

1978 was a particularly bitter winter and Ant fell ill with pneumonia. Despite his fortifying stout and Tegwyn's devoted nursing, a few months later, in February 1979, he died. He was forty years old and had earned himself a place in the *Guinness Book of Pet Records* as the oldest pit pony on record. Over the years Ant had acquired hundreds of friends, both children and adults, and when BBC Wales announced his death floral tributes and cards poured in. He was buried in the field where he'd lived out his golden years and a tree was planted to mark his grave.

In 1989 Italy lost almost its entire silk crop. The reason? A mysterious outbreak of greed that gripped the entire population of silkworm larvae. The larvae were so intent on chomping their way through tons of mulberry leaves that they couldn't be bothered to spin cocoons!

Crocodiles are built like submarines. Their bodies are streamlined, and valves close up the ears, nostrils, and windpipe when they submerge. A transparent third eyelid covers the eye. Although the crocodile is the world's largest reptile, its brain is just a little bigger than a man's thumb.

One of the largest gatherings of sea turtles ever seen occurred on Raine Island, part of Australia's Great Barrier Reef, in December 1984. Between 50,000 and 150,000 female green turtles congregated to lay up to 1,000 eggs each. In one night alone 11,500 turtles were counted.

# Rocky and Barco

Along the Texas border, in the Rio Grande Valley, illegal immigration and drug smuggling abound. The drug problem in particular is so bad that the area is known as Cocaine or Marijuana Alley. In the McAllen Sector there are two US Border Patrol checkpoints – the Sarita Station on Highway 77 and Falfurrias – operated by teams of specialized agents.

Central to their work are Rocky and Barco, two canine collaborators with the honorary rank of Sergeant Major. These fawn-red, three-year-old Belgian Malinois dogs, born and trained in Holland, are lovable, friendly and awesomely efficient. Since they started work in April 1987 they have been instrumental in making more than 250 narcotic seizures with a total value of £135.2 million. The media attention they continually attract has turned them into celebrities, a national symbol of America's fight against the drug scourge. It has also, however, put them high on the hit-list of those profiting from the trade in illegal narcotics. The Mexican smugglers who have lost enormous sums since Rocky and Barco's arrival on the scene have now put a £30,000 price on their heads.

One of Rocky's first successes concerned an eighteen-wheel articulated lorry that pulled up more than 25 yards from the Sarita Station. Even at that distance the dog sensed something was not right and a search uncovered

150 lb of marijuana. On another occasion Barco became suspicious of a huge water-carrying tanker. His hunch meant the agents had to cut the vehicle open with blow torches, hoping that the dog wasn't wrong. He wasn't. The moment Barco could get inside, he led them to a massive 700 lb of marijuana that had been skilfully stashed away.

---

In August 1985 hundreds of thousands of migrating toads hopped through the Chinese village of Wang-jianan, in Sichuan Province, on their way towards the hills. The procession was highly organized, divided into two lines about a foot apart, and took five days to pass.

---

# Michelle

On a blustery day in October 1988, Jan Morgan found a seal pup trapped in netting at a fish farm near Hillswick in the Shetlands. She disentangled the terrified creature and carried her back to the seal sanctury she'd established in the garden of her pub.

Michelle, as Jan named her, positively revelled in her status as pampered guest. She was loved, fed plenty of fish, and became wildly popular with regulars of The Booth. On Boxing Day, however, Jan reluctantly decided it was time for the pup to return to the freezing waters of the North Sea.

It was a sad farewell because Jan was sure she'd never see Michelle again. She was wrong as it turned out. A fortnight later she was working behind the bar when she heard loud mournful cries outside. She hurried to the door where, who should she see flapping laboriously up the steps, but Michelle. The seal pup had lost 20 lb and the eagerness she displayed clearly showed she thought she was coming home. Jan gave her a big welcome, a good feed of fish, and proceeded to nurse her back to full strength again.

Michelle's happiness was total, Jan's less so. She knew that, like it or not, the day would come when the pup would have to return to her natural habitat and rejoin others of her kind.

---

During the approach of Halley's comet in 1985, Thames Valley Eggs offered £5,000 for an egg with 'comet markings' on the shell. They received 350 entries – some marked with star shapes, speckled tails, lumps or ridges. The winning egg was submitted by Mr and Mrs Davies of Swansea and had 'a near-perfect circle with a halo around it – just like a planet surrounded by a haze'.

---

# Benji 1 and Benji 2

Benji, originally named Higgins, started life as an orphan puppy from the Burbank Animal Shelter and went on to become one of America's biggest canine stars. His career was launched in a TV series called *Petticoat Junction* and his later movies – the first grossing profits of £45 million – broke box office records in countries as diverse as Japan, Australia and Venezuela.

He was described as America's 'Most Huggable Hero' and the 'Laurence Olivier of the dog world'. A producer of Mulberry Square Productions, Dallas, is quoted as saying, 'Of course, we had Rin Tin Tin and Lassie, but really they were no more than props. In Benji's film it is the dog that acts, the co-stars are the props.'

When he eventually retired he was succeeded by his son,

Benji 2, who not only lived up to his father's reputation but outstripped it. Critics generally agreed that the new Benji was an even better actor than his distinguished father and his movies *For the Love of Benji* and *Oh Heavenly Dog* were smash hits. He also achieved world-wide fame and travelled to dozens of countries to meet his fans.

Benji 2 followed Lassie as the second animal to be inducted into the American Humane Society's Animal Actors' Hall of Fame, twice received the American Guild of Variety Artists' Georgie Award as the Top Animal Entertainer, and was voted one of the ten most popular performers in the United States.

---

In 1985 hundreds of fieldmice were reported to be committing suicide by jumping off cliffs in the Golan Heights or drowning themselves in streams. A nature expert at the nearby Keshet Field School explained the phenomenon as an instinctive response to overcrowding. There are around 250 fieldmice in the region.

---

# Choosy Cat

Snowy is a very choosy cat. She knows exactly what she likes – which is rabbit meat – and refuses to eat anything else. In 1983 her owner, Mrs Christine Cowton, bought four tins of unlabelled cat food from her local market on the assurance they contained 100% top quality rabbit meat. But when she served Snowy her supper that evening the cat took one mouthful then turned away in disgust. Mrs Cowton opened the next tin, then the third and the fourth, but Snowy turned her nose up disdainfully at them all.

To Mrs Cowton there was only one explanation – the

contents were not what they pretended to be. She called in consumer protection officials who confirmed the tins contained second quality beef!

Snowy's unfailing sense of taste and refusal to accept anything but the best landed the crooked trader a £450 fine. She also taught him never to underestimate his feline customers again.

> Chinese scientists were so convinced of the existence of ape-like wildmen in the region of Shennongjia, in Hubei Province, that a portion of the national park was designated a special reserve for them.

# The War Of The Sumatra Elephants

Attacks by wild elephants on rural communities in Sumatra, Indonesia, have increased sharply since the beginning of the 1980s. In April 1983, 115 elephants were moved from forests in south Sumatra to make way for a settlement. Shortly afterwards they broke through an electric fence and started trekking home, leaving a trail of destruction in their wake. A few months later a herd of twenty animals, well-known for their frequent attacks on villages, vented their fury on 200 acres of coconut trees.

In January 1984 another rogue herd broke out of a northern reserve and ran amok through 25 acres of marijuana, attacking the growers and sending them fleeing in terror. In November of the same year the village of Jawa, a thousand miles north-west of Jakarta, was stormed. Sixty trumpeting elephants suddenly burst out of the jungle, thundered through the muddy streets and flattened every single building before disappearing again. The villagers salvaged what possessions they could and fled to Rayeuk several miles away. Two months later the same herd attacked Rayeuk. They continued to return every afternoon for several days, trampling paddy fields and sending the people scurrying to the safety of a nearby hillside.

In 1985 seventeen elephants broke out of Bukit Barisan National Park and descended on the village of Sekinau. The inhabitants had prior warning of their approach and, with the help of police, managed to drive them away. The elephants returned three days later, however, destroyed twenty-three dwellings and trampled a young girl to death. Pujiyem Binti Karsimin's body was later discovered tossed into a paddy field.

One of the most ferocious attacks to be reported, though, occurred in 1986 when sixty of the frenzied beasts charged the Masuji Resettlement Centre, 250 miles north-east of Jakarta. They went on a murderous rampage that left fifteen villagers dead, dozens of houses flattened and extensive crops destroyed.

Why so many of Sumatra's 2,000 wild elephants have decided to wage war is a question preoccupying all Indonesians. Sumatra conservation officials say the savage attacks are the elephants' way of fighting the relentless encroachment of their habitat, mostly through the spread of illegal farming. As a man called Heathcote Williams said: 'There has never been an elephant "problem". There is no elephant "problem". There is only a human problem.'

---

When Mary Rossi died in 1986 she left twelve-year-old Minky £10,000 to keep her in style for the rest of her life. The guardians of this wealthy feline were expected to provide a menu which included poached cod in parsley sauce, boiled chicken with side portion of chopped livers and her favourite brand of tuna.

In 1988 Wayne Norgate went on holiday with his parents to Mablethorpe in Lincolnshire. He was happily paddling his 5 ft dinghy in the shallow waters near the beach when suddenly treacherous North Sea currents swept him out to sea. He huddled in the boat, helpless and weeping with fear while the figures on the beach grew smaller and smaller. Wayne was a mile from shore when help suddenly appeared. A seal surfaced next to the dinghy, grabbed a corner in its mouth and began pulling the boat back towards the shore. Meanwhile Wayne's parents had alerted the coastguards who raced to the scene. The seal stayed holding the dinghy until the men had got the boy safely aboard. Then, like a true hero, he disappeared.

# Barry

Barry was the most famous of the St Bernard rescue dogs bred at the Hospice du Grand St Bernard 81,000 feet above sea level in the Swiss Alps. Like others of his breed he had an astonishing sense of direction, a supreme ability to scent out bodies buried several feet deep under the snow, and a psychic awareness of impending disasters such as snowstorms and avalanches. He worked at the Hospice from 1800 to 1812 and is said to have saved the lives of more than forty people.

One of the most remarkable instances concerned a small boy left unconscious and half frozen to death after his mother had been killed by an avalanche. Barry lay across the child's body to restore his body heat, licked his face until he'd revived sufficiently to climb on his back, then carried him through deep snowdrifts to the Hospice.

One report said that Barry died after a young soldier he found dying in the snow mistook him for an attacking wolf and stabbed him with a knife; another that he was killed by an avalanche whilst on a rescue mission.

Happily neither were true. Barry was given a comfortable

retirement in Berne where he died of natural causes in 1814, and his stuffed body can be seen today at the Berne National History Museum.

The Hospice du Grand St Bernard was founded by St Bernard of Menthon in 1049. Since 1750 their rescue dogs have been credited with saving the lives of over 2,500 people.

---

Cockroaches have been around for at least 350 million years and are one of the most remarkable species alive. They can exist without food or water for a month, will eat anything, and a mating pair can produce 400,000 offspring a year. Because of their resistance to radiation, they are believed to be one of the few creatures which would survive a nuclear holocaust.

---

# The Surrey Puma

In January 1985 Bee Gee Maurice Gibb was watching television with his wife and children in their Esher home when his guard dogs suddenly tensed. He let them out and followed them into the garden. The dogs were halfway across the lawn when they froze abruptly. As Gibb stared in amazement a huge shape sprang out of the bushes, bounded across the drive and disappeared. Chessington Zoo experts arrived later to examine the animal's tracks, identifying them as belonging to a puma. Although Gibb didn't realize it at the time, he had made the 718th sighting of the legendary Surrey puma.

Described as the size of a large dog, black, with yellow eyes and a thick bushy tail, the Surrey puma first entered local folklore in the early sixties when it was spotted all over Hampshire, Sussex and Surrey. The reports weren't

The Tahitian bear dog is the rarest dog in the world. Only two are known to exist and they are both in Canada.

In 1980 it was revealed that the CIA had trained cats to carry bombs. This information, contained in documents released to the American public under the Freedom of Information Act, also showed that the CIA used otters to place underwater explosives and had carried out research on plants to see if they could communicate with – and give information about – people.

Spotty, a pint-sized Jack Russell terrier, is 10 in tall and weighs in at 12 lb. He shares his home – the Old Station Hotel in Giggleswick, North Yorks – with Cindy, a 10 st Rottweiler bitch, 20 in taller than himself. But despite this enormous difference in their sizes, Spotty somehow managed to mount Cindy and father a frisky pup, Lucky. His owner was flabbergasted by the feat, especially as the local vet had told him not to bother having Spotty doctored as he'd never be able to reach the towering Cindy. Speculation among the pub regulars is that, after lapping up a bowl of his favourite best bitter, Spotty performed the act standing on a beer crate!

In time of war, the animal kingdom's highest decoration is the Dickin Medal awarded by the PDSA for gallantry in the face of the enemy. During the Second World War it was awarded to eighteen dogs, three horses, thirty-one pigeons and one ship's cat.

Dawn Rogers is an animal preacher in California, USA, with a mail order Minister's licence from the Universal Life Church. She specializes in formalizing the union between animals and in 1986 had already conducted seventeen marriage ceremonies. Among those creatures who tied the knot at her altar were cats, dogs, goldfish, horses and even a pair of amorous frogs. Her weddings cost anything up to £200.

taken seriously, however, until August 1964 when a Friesian bullock was found lacerated near the village of Crodall.

At the same time a local farmer claimed he was being kept awake at night by 'the most unearthly shrieking wail', said by knowledgeable old colonials to be the cry of the deer tiger puma. The villagers, armed to the teeth with shotguns and sharpened staves, organized a stake-out but failed to find the beast which, it later transpired, had moved on to neighbouring Munstead Heath.

More than 150 sightings were reported during the next few months, all dutifully entered in a special puma ledger kept by Surrey police. The collective imagination was fired and safaris were being organized into Reigate, Farnham, Stoke Poges and Slough.

By the early seventies the Surrey puma had changed many of its habits. Most importantly it no longer stalked sheep and roe deer, preferring to rifle the dustbins of affluent Surrey residents instead. On one occasion it was disturbed by the daughter of Lord Chelmsford, Philippa Thesiger, as it lurked near refuse containers at Hazelbridge Court, Godalming. Instead of running off when it saw her, it crouched ready to pounce and she had to beat it off with a walking stick.

The second half of the seventies and early eighties were quiet as far as the Surrey puma was concerned, although sightings of a similar creature were reported in Wales, Exmoor, Renfrewshire and Scotland where a huge cat-like creature reportedly 'terrorized an Alsatian dog'. It resurfaced in 1983, however, with fourteen sightings, seven of them in Essex and three near Stokenchurch, High Wycombe. By 1984 it was being spotted all over mid-Surrey, sometimes in the winding lanes and coppices, more often prowling the gardens of the stockbroker belt and pilfering from the dustbins.

A few years later a strange wild cat that didn't conform to any known species was shot and killed. Many say it was the famous Surrey 'puma'.

# The Terrible Blob

In 1983 *The New York Times* reported the existence of a terrible, and hitherto unknown, blob with the name of *Dictostelium caveatum*. *Dictostelium caveatum*, discovered by a Princeton biologist in an Arkansas cavern, is a ferociously aggressive slime mould that grazes on bat excrement. The nasty mould is a coalition of amoebas and behaves like a single slug-like animal. It dispatches 'attack' amoebas to infiltrate a prey species of slime mould and, once inside, the predators multiply and eat up their hosts. As cell by cell is devoured the victims are changed from prey species to predator *caveatum*. One can't help wondering if the awesome *Dictostelium caveatum* will obliterate all the other slime moulds in the world to become Slime Blob supreme?

For eleven years a black Labrador called Emma was Sheila Hocken's devoted guide dog. Then in 1978 Sheila, blind since birth, underwent an operation that restored her sight. Almost simultaneously, something very bizzare happened. Emma developed cataracts and shortly afterwards went blind herself. Sheila looked after Emma as lovingly as Emma had looked after her – she became the 'guide person' of her dog.

# Roy

One of the most extraordinary and difficult animal rescues ever reported was carried out by an Alsatian called Roy. It was a feat that required, not only courage, but an awareness of the precise nature of the danger and a high degree of intelligent reasoning. The incident occurred in Sweden in May 1977.

Leif Rongemo had been playing with his two-year-old daughter, Annelli, in the sitting room of his flat when he left her briefly with the dog to get something from the kitchen. He was only gone a few minutes but when he returned the room was empty and the window wide open. Sick with dread, he forced himself to walk over to the window and stare down the dizzying 36 ft into the street below. But no little body lay lifeless on the pavement.

His relief was very short-lived, however. Glancing to his left, he saw his baby daughter crawling on all fours along the narrow ledge that ran around the building – and, behind her, creeping on his belly, was Roy.

It was a heart-stopping moment. Leif realized that if he shouted, or startled them in any way, both would plunge to their deaths as the ledge was too narrow for either of them to turn. He rushed into the other room to break the terrible news to his wife. While she made an hysterical call to the fire brigade, Leif ran downstairs with a neighbour and positioned himself below the block of flats with an outstretched blanket.

Meanwhile Roy had continued to inch along behind the toddler. When he got within striking distance, he suddenly made a swift decisive movement and seized the child's nappy in his jaws. Leif and the neighbour watched with bated breath as the Alsatian, with extreme caution, proceeded to shuffle backwards towards the window.

It took three agonizing minutes before a distraught Mrs Rongemo was able to grab hold of Annelli and snatch her to safety. Only then did Roy give a triumphant wag of his tail and jump back inside himself.

---

In November 1988 two shipwrecked sailors floundering in rough seas off the coast of Indonesia were nudged and guided to the safety of a small island by a school of dolphins. Once on dry land they were able to raise the alarm which resulted in nine other crew members being plucked out of the sea.

---

# Sky Raiders

In 1984 the Lapp village of Idre in Sweden was being terrorized by a predatory eagle of phenomenal strength. The bird became such a problem to the reindeer herds that the villagers petitioned for permission to shoot it, a request that was refused because the golden eagle is a protected species.

Sigvard Jonsson, the village spokesman, claimed that he had seen the eagle carry off a six-month-old reindeer calf, watching in amazement as it transported the 55 lb weight for almost 200 metres before dropping it. The eagle's record of devastation was gory. It had already carried off ten young reindeer and had learned to kill the bigger heifers, which it could not lift, by biting into the carotid artery.

In August 1984 a Finnish newspaper the Helsinki

'Stop kidding around . . .' two kid goats play with a golden
labrador. *Oxford Scientific Films – John Cooke*

'What shall we play?' the Jack Russell asks the hedgehog.
*Oxford Scientific Films – Mike Birkhead*

Gerenuk feeding on an acacia bush.
*Oxford Scientific Films – Richard Packwood*

*Ilta-Sanomat* carried the report of the attempted abduction of a three-year-old girl by a hawk. Tina Lamminen was playing in the courtyard of her grandmother's house in Liljendhal, near Loviisa on the south coast of Finland, when a hawk appeared in the sky and began circling watchfully. When the child went back inside to play in the living room, it suddenly dived, crashing through the 3 mm thick glass and seizing her head in its talons. Tina's mother came rushing into the room, grabbed the bird and hurled it against the wall. The stunned bird was then killed by the child's uncle.

In 1986 a 6 lb Siamese cat named Blackie was snatched from a garden in Droxford, near Portsmouth, by a huge bird with a wingspan so large it covered the cat completely. It carried Blackie for several yards until the cat's frantic struggling became too unmanageable and it dropped him. Frank Voysey of the local Royal Society for the Protection of Birds said the predator was almost certainly a buzzard.

In July 1986 a gourmet restaurant for upper class dogs was inaugurated in Florida, USA. Among the six VIP canines invited to Coco's Sidewalk Café's opening bash was a five-year-old white Maltese called Omar. Omar, who sleeps on monogrammed sheets in a brass bed and has his nails done twice a month, turned up in stunning red pyjamas with matching ribbon in his hair. He scoffed down three plates of beef tartare, a helping of chopped turkey breast and washed the lot down with a bowl of Evian water. Coco's doggie menu costs a mere $5.75 and offers a choice of rare roast beef, turkey or raw ground beef and a selection of bottled mineral waters. It also provides 'people bags' for owners to take home any tasty left-overs.

# Unsung Heroes

Throughout history and all over the world the canine attributes of intelligence, loyalty and courage have been exploited by the military. The ancient Romans forced them to swallow metal tubes containing messages which they then had to deliver across miles of battle-torn territory. Their courage was never rewarded, however. On reaching their destinations, the animals were barbarically killed and their bellies slit open so the commanders could get at the message.

During World War I, 1,500 highly trained dogs served in the German army, and the French had dogs working with their infantry regiments. Entirely dependable, however nerve-racking the conditions, these animals could cover difficult terrain in minutes (compared to hours for a man) and provided a much smaller and more swiftly moving target.

Towards the end of 1916 Colonel Edward Richardson established the world-famous War Dog School on the south coast of England, eventually training dogs not only for the army, but also for the police.

During World War I, 7,000 dogs were killed in action, and many more died from firearm wounds and poison gas. They were Alaskan huskies, Alsatians, sheepdogs, Airedales, terriers, lurchers and a host of shabby mongrels, nearly all strays from Dogs' Homes. And most of them died unsung heroes, mourned only by their handlers.

---

In 1973 a guide dog called Sally sacrificed her life to save her blind master. The golden Labrador was hit by a car as she pushed her 79-year-old master, Bill Chamberlain, on to the pavement of a busy street to stop him being run over.

# Bill and Crystal

In 1973 engineering student Bill Powell had an accident
which left him a quadriplegic – someone who cannot move
their arms or legs. He was told his injuries were so severe
he'd have to spend the rest of his life in a nursing home.
But four years later he met Dr Mary Joan Willard, a young
medical researcher in New England, USA, who was
interested in experimenting with monkeys to see if they
could be trained to function as the hands, arms and legs of
paralysis victims. She persuaded him to move into a room
on the sixth floor of her institute and together they would
work with a monkey called Crystal.

For the first few months Bill and Crystal just concentrated on getting to know each other. She had a lively,
wilful personality and untrained was a real handful. One
day Bill and Dr Willard returned to the room to find she
had escaped from her cage and turned both the bath taps
on. Not content with merely flooding the place, she had
also thrown all Bill's books on the floor.

She was trained on her favourite treat of raisins, her
reward when she got something right. But being a very
bright little monkey, she also found ways of getting them
anyway. On one occasion she distracted Bill by pulling his
hair with one hand, while surreptitiously probing his
pocket with the other. Five minutes later he discovered the
little devil had taken a packet of raisins and a cigar.

They had plenty of personality clashes along the way,

too, but eventually Crystal learned who was boss. She became a totally devoted one-man monkey, performing all the hundreds of manual tasks that Bill couldn't do for himself, such as switching on and off lights, all manner of fetching and carrying, lighting his cigar and even scratching his nose.

After the success with Crystal and Bob, Dr Willard began training other monkeys, her long-term aim being to open a school able to match monkeys to quadriplegics and provide an alternative to round-the-clock helpers and attendants.

When in 1983 a sick orphaned otter was taken to an animal sanctuary near Beith, Ayrshire, it was immediately adopted by Tangle, the Sanctuary's pet spaniel. The mother-love she lavished on the pathetic, ailing creature was the principal reason for its eventual recovery. In the past Tangle has been 'mother' to a baby deer, two fox cubs and several rabbits.

# Congo

Salvador Dali rated him higher than Jackson Pollock; Pablo Picasso expressed great appreciation when he was presented with one of his paintings; and Joan Miro made a special trip to secure a canvas for himself. The artist in question was a chimpanzee named Congo who shot to fame in the 1950s when he became a regular on *Zoo-Time*, a weekly TV programme hosted by Desmond Morris.

His first efforts were primitive and not very interesting scribbles but, with Morris's encouragement, he went on to develop a valid and individual style. His exhibition at a

London gallery became a talking point in the art world. Success didn't go to his head, though. He continued to live at London Zoo and dedicate himself to his art.

On 10 September 1985 John Brice wrote the following letter to *The Times*: 'Recent observations of the travelling habits of London's feral pigeon population suggests a level of intelligence hitherto unsuspected. Using the district line, I have seen pigeons boarding the underground trains at Edgware Road station and later alight at various points along the line. Fulham Broadway and Parson's Green seem to be favoured and also Putney Bridge if it is low water.'

# Toffee and Jo-Jo

Toffee is a golden brown part-Labrador who lives with her master, Kevin Roche, in the West Indies. In 1987 they were on one of their regular sailing trips together when the dog spotted a dolphin frolicking ten yards or so away. With a delighted bark he jumped into the water and paddled over to say hello. Dog looked at dolphin, dolphin looked at dog and they both decided they liked each other.

The two animals have met every day since and their affection for each other has grown with every encounter. The basis of their friendship is a mutual and spontaneous love of play – they don't work at communicating, they just enjoy a ripping good game. Their romps always start with the same ritual. Jo-Jo, as the dolphin was later named, greets Toffee's arrival with high joyful leaps. Toffee responds with excited barks, jumps into the water and gives chase. Jo-Jo goes along with this for a while, then suddenly turns the tables on her pursuer, swims underneath him to resurface in a glistening shower of drops a foot away.

They then proceed to splash, jump, chase and dive like a couple of boisterous children until Kevin decides it's time to go home and calls the reluctant dog away. Toffee stands on the deck watching the dolphin trailing the boat. Then, with a farewell leap, Jo-Jo disappears until their next meeting the following day.

> Burt is not an ordinary duck. He waddles onto the stage, turns to the tiny white piano and, with a quick flick of his white tails, starts an impeccable rendering of a Chopin melody. Burt is one of the many animals, that include turkeys, dolphins, reindeer, cows and snakes, that have been trained by an outfit called Animal Behavior Enterprises. Not all their animals are trained to entertain. Some are involved in much more serious, and highly secret, projects.

# Pikki

Pikki was a small fox terrier bitch belonging to a Russian animal trainer, Vladimir Durov. She was by far the most remarkable of his troupe of circus dogs, able to pick up mentally transmitted commands. News of her extraordinary telepathic ability reached the ears of a well-known neurologist of the day, Professor Vladimir Bechterev, who asked Durov if he would bring Pikki to his offices to be studied.

In the series of tests, which were conducted just before the outbreak of World War I, great care was taken to avoid gestures or facial expressions that would give the dog clues. Pikki had an almost hundred per cent success rate in tests where she was asked telepathically to pick up objects from the floor, jump on a table, point to a certain picture with her paw, collect sheet music from the piano or pull something out of a drawer.

On one occasion she was mentally ordered to ferociously attack a large toy wolf in the corner of the room, and she complied with gusto. Professor Bechterev, however, had noticed that Durov's expression had been very intense when he gave the command and, thinking that might have influenced Pikki, decided to repeat the test the next day. On the second occasion Durov kept his face relaxed and smiling while he mentally transmitted the command, but the ferocity of Pikki's attack was in no way diminished.

One of the interesting things to come out of the test was that Pikki's telepathic ability was not exclusively confined to Durov. She was able to pick up mental instructions from Professor Bechterev and his assistants too. She also performed well when the instructions were transmitted from another room, and carried them out in the presence of people who were completely unaware that any testing was going on at all.

In October 1984 police in Beebe, Arkansas, USA, received a distress call which was eventually traced to a closed warehouse. When the officers arrived, however, they discovered that the caller was a terrier called Frazzles who'd somehow managed to get trapped inside. According to the amused cops, the clever canine had knocked the receiver off the hook and pushed the 'panic' button with his paw. This immediately connected him to the local police station where he barked out his plight. It had taken police three hours to locate the call, during which time the line had been tied up and unavailable to other emergency callers.

# Silvermere Haven

When Pam Gilbert's fifteen-year-old tabby died ten years ago she was buried in the family's garden. It was a very sad loss and made her aware of the fact that a great many people had nowhere special they could bury their dearly loved pets. So, together with her husband Mike, she decided to turn 11 acres of land bought as an investment into a pet cemetery which they called Silvermere Haven. There are now over 2,000 dear departeds at Silvermere and include not only dogs and cats, which make up the majority, but also snakes, birds, a tortoise and even a monkey.

A plot at Silvermere costs anything from £40 for a cat to £120 for an extra large dog. Cremations – which are the most popular – are £25 for a cat plus £20 for a plot, £15 for the casket and £5 for the stone. The annual maintenance fee is £5 for cremation plots and £10 for burial plots. Silvermere will also collect the pet from home and retains several acres for communal burials.

Funerals range from the simple to the very grand. A dog can be buried in his favourite blanket or in a sumptuous, satin-lined casket under an elaborately engraved marble headstone. People come with many odd requests. One man wanted his dog to be buried with a slice of cheese and a bag of chocolate buttons; another was buried with the brand of potato crisps that had been his passion, yet another was put to rest wearing a silk scarf and her nose tucked into her favourite slipper.

There is a poignancy to the expanse of tiny plots and headstones with sad little epitaphs: 'Scruffy – our little sausage. Will love you always'. 'Pepi – a broken link that can never be replaced. Mummy and Auntie'. 'Whisky. Runaway Winkway. 18.7.66 – 29.12.81. Missed by all the family. Love Mum and Dad'.

But it's not only the eccentric or the childless who bring their pets to be buried at Silvermere Haven. Three police handlers have buried their dogs in plots marked by imposing headstones, so has a tattooed skinhead and a close aide of Margaret Thatcher. Dai Llewellyn, erstwhile beau of Princess Margaret, interred his dog there too. The message on the gravestone reads: 'Cosmos – a gentleman. Help me live without you'.

> In the eighteenth century a creature variously described as a rabid wolf, a hyena or a panther terrorized the Cevennes Mountains of south-west France. Popularly known as the Wild Beast of Gevaudan, it killed an estimated 64–100 people between 1764 and 1767.

# Caesar

The hurricane that swept through Northern Europe in November 1972 was at its howling height when Anna Buck, a widow, imprudently left her farmhouse to feed the chickens. She had only walked a few paces, however, when her pet St Bernard, Caesar, rushed out after her, barking furiously. He seized the hem of her coat in his teeth and dragged her back inside the house. She had only just made it to the door when tiles and masonry ripped from the roof by the 100 miles per hour wind crashed to the very spot she would have been standing.

It was an extraordinary example of the psychic ability to see the future that animals so often prove they possess. Caesar was awarded West Germany's highest valour award for dogs – a gold medal from the animal rescue society.

---

In 1987 New Yorker Mickey Bonhannon discovered that feeding his six-year-old pet elephant could be even more expensive than he'd reckoned. One day Butch put his trunk through a window of Mickey's house, snatched an envelope and ate it. The envelope contained $1,000.

---

# The Monster of Labinkir

The Siberian equivalent of our own 'Nessie' is called the Monster of Labinkir. It is said to lurk in the freezing waters of Lake Labinkir, 150 miles south of the gold-mining town of Ust-Nera in the province of Yakutia.

Although there had been many stories of its existence, the first reliable sightings were made in the 1950s. One of them came from a group of geologists who were working at the lakeside when they were distracted by loud splashing. They stared in astonishment as a long-necked animal emerged from the murky lake, uttered a 'sound much like a child's cry', and disappeared into the frigid depths again. A second group of geologists on a field expedition in the same area claimed to have seen the outline of its greyish body through the thin ice. About the same time a team of reindeer hunters alleged they had witnessed the monster lunge out of the water to snap up a low-flying bird.

An article on the mysterious creature appeared in *Komsomolskaya Pravada* in the 1960s. It stirred up a lot of interest and many expeditions were formed to investigate. All of them, however, failed to get even the most fleeting glimpse. Soviet biologists say that the Monster of Labinkir is probably just a giant schuka or northern pike, fishes which can reach up to 9 ft in length.

> Joseph Banks Rhine, one of the foremost scientists studying animal Extra Sensory Perception (ESP) in America, has collected five hundred examples of animal behaviour that overwhelmingly indicate ESP. The main areas he's been investigating are: 1) The Ability to sense the master's unexpected return. 2) Sensing imminent danger. 3) Sensing a master's death over a distance. 4) The ability to return home across unknown territory. 5) The ability to trace owners who've moved to a new home.

# Rob
# War Dog No 471/322

Rob, otherwise known as War Dog No 471/322, served with the Special Air Service (SAS) in North Africa and Italy. He worked with SAS raiding parties that were parachuted behind enemy lines to sabotage their emplacements. It was work that demanded exceptional courage and nerves of steel and on numerous occasions he was able to save his comrades' lives by giving timely warnings of approaching German or Italian patrols.

Wearing a specially designed harness, Rob made more than twenty parachute jumps with the SAS, never once hesitating or showing any fear when his turn came to launch himself through the hatch of the aircraft into the void. Throughout his active service his courage never faltered and he was a continual inspiration to all the soldiers he worked alongside.

Fortunately he survived the war and in January 1945 the black-and-white mongrel was presented with the Dickin Medal, the animal kingdom's highest wartime award for bravery in the face of the enemy.

> Soviet news reports allege there is a talking raven near Minsk, who flies around the river inspecting anglers' catches and telling them exactly what fish they've caught.

# Rat Stories

American journalist George Law began collecting rat stories in 1988. He put an ad in New York's *Village Voice* asking people to write to him with their experiences and got some amazing – if horrific – replies.

A man called Jon reported catching a rat in a trap he'd laid in his kitchen. He walked in to find the wily rodent edging the contraption against the leg of the table, nudging it until the catch mechanism sprang and released its neck. As Jon gaped in disbelief, the rat flicked its tail and sauntered off.

Then there was the grisly experience of the woman, woken in the night by a sharp pain in her face, who found a rat sitting on her pillow, about to make a meal out of her nose.

There were also several stories about rats surfacing in toilet bowls, the most chilling from Jenny who lives on New York's Upper East Side. She recounted how her mother was sitting on the toilet when she heard a splashing sound and a second later felt something wet and hairy nuzzling her bare bottom. She screamed, jumped into the air, tore off all her clothes and dived into the shower. A few minutes later she mustered her courage to venture another look and found herself staring into a pair of beady black eyes. A R Tatum, a pest-control man from Augusta, Georgia, wrote with similar stories of two women living in different parts of a Southern city who'd both been bitten on their rear ends while sitting on the loo. The problem apparently occurred with sufficient frequency for an Omaha company to market a 'plastic rodent stopper' that 'clasps the toilet in such a way that when the toilet is flushed, its tongue allows water and waste matter to flow out, but will not allow anything that might have crawled up a sewer pipe to pass the barrier'.

There are an estimated 30 million rats in the city of New York. They can grow to 17 in (including tail), reach 1 lb in weight and are even said to be able to survive nuclear explosions. They gnaw all day long because if they didn't their chisel-edged upper incisors would grow at the rate of four inches a year, curling round and up through the palate and into the brain. And they can gnaw through almost everything: plastics, lead pipes, even concrete walls. Rats like all things human, including their adornments. They have been known to drag lipsticks, rings, keys, banknotes and assorted bric-à-brac into their nests. The rat is a determined survivor, now able to tolerate 100 times the dose of poison that once would have killed him and, next to man himself, is the most adaptable creature on Earth.

There have been periods in their history, however, when some cultures have taken a more kindly view of the rodent than we do. The Indians associated it with prosperity, commonly depicting the God Ganesha riding on a rat steed. The Chinese believed that rat flesh – which is supposed to taste like rabbit – stopped hair loss. They made it more palatable by selling it at markets flattened out and dried. Filipino chefs even made a rat sausage – and considered it a delicacy!

When Lord Thompson, one of Britain's first Air Ministers, boarded the airship R101 his normally inseparable terrier refused to go with him. The dog ran away and Lord Thompson went alone. Shortly after take-off, however, the airship crashed in what is one of the best remembered tragedies in the history of British aviation. The terrier, who had refused to eat and been nervous since early morning, obviously sensed the impending disaster.

# Jean Ricord and Coco

Jean Ricord and her ageing mongrel, Coco, were inseparable. Every day they took long leisurely walks around their neighbourhood of Nice, France, pausing every now and then to chat with an acquaintance or local shopkeeper.

Jean was a sprightly 59-year-old when, out of the blue, tragedy struck. She had a sudden, massive heart attack and died immediately. Coco's grief was terrible. For a whole week she languished on the balcony of the fourth floor apartment belonging to a friendly neighbour who had taken her in. She refused all food, hardly drank, gazing mournfully down at the street where she and her mistress had taken so many happy strolls.

On the seventh day Jean's funeral procession drove slowly past on its way to the cemetery. The moment she saw it Coco sprang to life – almost as though she'd been waiting for it all the time. She gave one small yelp before hurling herself off the balcony and plunging to her death.

Once they'd recovered from the shock, the mourners recognized that the old dog had killed herself because separation from her mistress was too painful to bear. It was decided to open the coffin there and then and place the broken little body inside. Coco had got her wish – she was reunited with Jean Ricord forever.

On 28 March 1903 a very curious banquet was held at Louis Sherry's elegant New York City restaurant. The novelty of the occasion was that all of the formally attired gentlemen who had been invited to attend were on horseback. Sod had been laid over the floor, feedbags were used instead of dinner plates and champagne was served out of rubber buckets.

# Lola and Rolf

Lola and her father, Rolf, were Airedale terriers famous for their mastery of arithmetic and the alphabet. Trained by their owner, Henny Jutzler-Kindermann, they tapped out simple sums with their paws and compiled words by using the corresponding numbers for letters. Lola was also able to forecast the weather and, after succumbing to the attentions of an amorous male, correctly predicted the number of puppies she would produce. Rolf shared his daughter's ability to see the future – in 1914 he is said to have given warning of the impending Mannheim earthquake.

Replying 'Wag your tail', to a woman who asked if there was anything she could do for him, it seems he had a waggish sense of humour too!

A flea can hop about 6 in into the air and cover as much as 2 ft in a single leap. Weight for weight, this is equivalent of a man leaping a quarter of a mile in just one bound. The animal long jump record was established in 1968 by a red kangaroo from New South Wales, Australia, who jumped 42 ft. The high jump record goes to an Australian red kangaroo, too. In 1968 it successfully sailed over a 10 ft high stack of wood.

# Stupid Sheep?

In 1984 farmers in South Wales had a problem. Their sheep had learned to roll bodily over cattle control grids to avoid getting their feet trapped in the metal bars and in less than two weeks had figured out how to get inside special 'sheep-proof' dustbins. Once out of their enclosures those that survived the hazards of passing motorists were joining up with stray ponies, and Wild West-type round-ups were needed to recapture them. A working party was set up to find new ways of outwitting the sheep. As the then Welsh Under-Secretary commented, 'We're dealing with a very ingenious and sophisticated animal around here.'

> A Plymouth man walked out on his wife when she turned their bedroom into a tropical habitat for some of her 100 spiders, snakes and frogs.

# Arnold Ziffel

Arnold Ziffel was a small, multi-talented Chester White pig who starred with Eva Gabor in the American TV series *Green Acres*. His many impressive accomplishments included playing the piano, collecting letters from a mail box, sipping drinks daintily through a straw, pulling a little wagon and generally being cute and adorable. The viewers absolutely loved him and Arnold Ziffel fan-clubs were formed all over the country. Some of his more devoted followers declared that love of Arnold had inspired them to give up eating pork.

The high point of his career came in 1968 and 1969 when,

for two years running, he carried off the American Humane Association's Paisy award for performing animals. But success was not kind to Arnold's waistline. In 1971 he was dropped from the series because gluttony had made him too fat for the part.

In 1989 an Angora goat-unicorn was on display at Marine World near San Francisco. The goat, whose name was Lancelot, had a ten-inch horn growing out of his forehead. Animal scientists said he wasn't a new species, just a 'rare abnormality'.

# Trooper

Ten-week-old Ian Curtiss was alone with the family's pet dog, Trooper, when a blaze started. The flames spread rapidly, eating up the soft furnishings and thick-pile carpet.

Instinctively knowing what he had to do, Trooper lay across the baby's body to shield him from the encroaching flames and when Ian's mother burst in she found them encircled by a ring of fire. Trooper's protective instinct was so strong that, despite his badly scorched fur, she had to kick him before he would move and let her carry the baby to safety.

In July 1983 Katrina the cat was taken by her owners to a vet in Pleaston, California, to be put down. She was given a lethal injection and her corpse put in a deep freeze. Two days later, however, Katrina turned up at her old home two miles away. The vet was totally astounded by her miraculous resurrection and could give no logical explanation for what had happened.

# First Cousins?

In California in the mid-seventies scientists mated a strand of DNA (the 'building block' of the cell) to its chimpanzee counterpart, creating the basis of a 'manchimp' or 'human-zee'. In doing so they were amazed to discover that man only differs from the chimp in 1.1% of his genetic material and also that his protein structure is practically identical to the apes'.

Long-term field study of chimps has demonstrated that they use their natural intelligence in their natural habitats as well as in laboratory conditions. They make frequent use of tools, carrying them for distances up to half a mile which involves the ability to mentally plan ahead. Chimps discovered, for example, that the best way for extracting the termites they like so much from termite hills is to use a stick and parents teach this skill to their offspring. Scientists observing chimpanzees in captivity found they were capable of recognizing themselves in a mirror without any training – an ability hitherto thought to be exclusively human. Moreover, if the mirror were left in the cage the chimp soon started using it to groom himself.

Then, in the early 1970s, scientific findings indicated that the great apes actually possess some of the higher intellectual abilities needed for reading. Reading requires the ability to recognize or match in one sense (say by touch) what has earlier been experienced by another sense (say by sight). This is something humans do with the greatest of ease. We can all, for example, identify coins or objects in our pockets without having to look. In the experiment to test this ability, the ape would first be given three objects. One of them was in a window and he could only look at it but not touch. The other two could not be looked at, only touched. One of these two was identical to the object in the window, the other was totally different. The ape had to reach through an opening in the box where these two objects were kept, feel them, then select the object that corresponded to the one he'd seen in the window. The result was 90% accuracy. A variety of conveniently small objects like screws, rattles, combs, etc, were used and when photographs were substituted for the objects themselves the animals did just as well.

The great apes possess the biggest brains of any primates apart from Man. Their disconcerting resemblance to us promoted the Dutch ethologist, Adriaan Kortlandt, to say: 'They are not people, but they are actually not animals either.'

In March 1986 a female tiger due to be slaughtered and its meat sold as a magical aphrodisiac was bought for £5,000 by priests who claimed they had 'converted it to Buddhism'. The priests later sent the animal to Kaohsiung Zoo to spread the word among the other animals there.

A fourteen-year-old female hamadryad baboon living at the Wild Animal Retirement Village in Florida, USA, just loves all cats. Since her arrival at the village she's mothered thirty kittens, the latest being Patches, Boots and Tiger born to another cat she had raised. The mother cat allows the baboon to do everything for her babies – except breast feed them.

Four-year-old Tammy Stokes was paddling in the shallow waters at EMU Park, Queensland, Australia, when a 10 ft shark swam inshore and attacked her. While everybody looked on paralysed with fear, a little mongrel called Dollar leapt to her rescue. The brave dog courageously tackled the enormous predator, snarling and snapping to keep it at bay until Tammy's father was able to snatch her to safety.

# Poor Dogs

This article, quoted in Gloria Cottesloe's book *The Story of The Battersea Dogs' Home* appeared in an 1867 publication called 'Aunt Judy's Christmas Volume for Young People' and gives a vivid picture of the life of strays in Victorian London:

'They will work for us, and die for us, and, after we are dead, lie on our graves for months, or even years. They have done so. So are we not bound to treat them well and kindly, better than all other creatures, for the love and service they give us so gladly? So have begun to think lately some kind people in London where dogs' misery, like human misery, reaches its worst limits. But the dogs have not been drinking nasty spirits, or spending their bread-money on tobacco, or doing everything they ought not to, like most of those poor masters of theirs. The dogs' troubles are never their own fault. And yet there they are by hundreds, in those endless streets of huge London, starving and without shelter, till their misery ends by their dying in some lonely corner into which they have crept. You can hardly go down a great street in London without seeing one or more of these miserable creatures. Sometimes it is a curled-up mass of dirty fur on the mat by a shop door, so still that it might be dead, but for the convulsive shiver now and then. It is generally a mere mass of skin and bone, and lies there trying to sleep away its hunger and misery. Speak to it, and it looks up with so wistful and imploring a look, that you cannot bear to leave it without doing anything for it. And yet, what can be done? You cannot adopt every cur-casual tramper dog you come across. A short time ago, it would have been very difficult to know what to do; but, thanks to those kind people I have alluded to, there really is now something to be done. The homeless and starving dogs have got a place to go to, if they only knew it, where they will be taken in and "done for", as lodging-house people say, if only some one would please to put them in the way of getting there.'

The 'place to go' was the newly founded Battersea Dogs' Home. The article also quotes the printed petition tied to the collar of a Battersea dog going to his or her new master:

'The Petition of the Poor Dog to his new Master or Mistress upon his Removal from the Home. Pray have a little patience with me. There are so many of us shut up together here that the keeper has no opportunity to teach us habits of cleanliness. I am quite willing to learn, and am quite capable of being taught. All that is necessary is, that you should take a little pain with me, and kindly bear with me until I have acquired such habits as you wish. I will then be your best and most faithful friend.'

The Pesut, who resemble well-fed babies with chubby necks, huge round heads and toothless gums, are believed to be the first new species of dolphin found in thirty-four years. Discovered in a remote river in Borneo, the Pesut shares many characteristics with its more streamlined relative: it's very good natured and trusting and happily accepts food from humans. The big difference is its lack of visible teeth which has resulted in its developing a curious feeding technique. The Pesut spurts a powerful jet of water to stun prey, then sucks the food through its immensely strong, gummy jaws.

Eighteenth century English philosopher, Jeremy Bentham, had little respect for his fellow humans considering most of them a waste of time. The only creature he really valued was his cat, Langbourne. He first addressed him as 'Sir John Langbourne', later elevating his status to 'The Reverend Sir John Langbourne'.

If an ape has a dirty mark on its face and is put in front of a mirror, it will immediately start rubbing its own face rather than its mirror image. Science historian, Adrian Desmond, claims that this proves apes are the only creatures other than man to have an awareness of 'image of self'.

Belka and Strelka, two female huskies, were the first animals to survive orbital flight. The Soviet Union launched them in Sputnik V on 19 August 1960. The dogs clocked up just over seventeen orbits in twenty-five hours.

Marine biologists have identified some twenty different dolphin sounds. Some appear to be warning cries, some call-signs so each animal can be recognized at a distance by their companions, others designed to keep the school together when travelling at speed. So far nobody has found evidence of dolphins putting together two sounds to make a sentence as, for example, chimpanzees do.

In 1985 a python called Snoopy was sacked during a Tyneside tour of a comedy play called *Strippers*. The reason? During the six week tour he'd grown from 5 ft long to 7 ft 6 in and was too big for the actress Jackie Lye to handle.

Tyson is an eleven stone, nine-month-old bull mastiff who hit the newspapers for being an absolute tearaway. During his short life he has chewed up his owner's carpet, eaten a wage packet containing £200 and smashed the TV. He also playfully sat on his mistress' mother and kept her pinned to the floor for a whole hour.

# Bobbie's 5,000 Mile Trek Home

The extraordinary adventure of a part English shepherd, part collie, called Bobbie began in August 1923 when he lost his owner while on holiday in Indiana. Frank Brazier searched long and hard for his pet but eventually had to return to Silverton in Oregon where he ran a restaurant. He was convinced that he would never see his dog again. But early one morning six months later Bobbie limped up the stairs to the apartment above the restaurant, jumped onto the bed and began licking Frank's face. He was thin, exhausted and the pads of his paws were so consumed that the bone showed through. He had travelled 5,000 kilometres and overcome countless hardships to find his way home.

Bobbie's journey was reconstructed by the president of the Oregon Humane Society who took testimonies from the many people who'd fed and sheltered him along the way. Initially, he discovered, Bobbie had gone round in circles, disorientated and unable to get his bearings, and it wasn't until the autumn that he was finally on the right track. Moving west, never stopping more than two or three days in any one place, he travelled through Illinois and Iowa. His route took him through towns, cities, over the formidable Rocky Mountains, across streams and rivers –

including the huge Missouri which during the winter was treacherous with floating blocks of ice.

For the rest of his life Bobbie was a much-fêted local hero.

In a chilling experiment investigating animal Extra Sensory Perception (ESP), Russian scientists planted electrodes in the head of a mother rabbit and wired her up to a 'brain wave machine'. Her six babies were meanwhile taken to a submarine hundreds of miles away and, after submersion, killed one by one. Back in the Moscow laboratory the mother rabbit's brain waves showed violent disturbance at the exact moment each one of her babies were killed.

# Dessie

Desert Orchid (also known as The Flying Grey, the Wonder Horse and the Knight's Charger) is deliriously described as having a noble head, enormous dark liquid eyes, long lean nose and white silken hair that falls into an irresistibly romantic forelock. But the ten-year-old horse is not only beautiful, he's also one of the greatest and most versatile steeplechasers ever. On 16 March 1989 he won his 27th race to take the Gold Cup at Cheltenham, making an epic struggle through the mud which everybody agreed put him up with the immortals.

This unrivalled heart-throb of the horsey world has a large devoted following, which includes an unofficial fan club of young girls sporting 'We Love Dessie' sweaters. Before the Cheltenham race, Tracy and Jenny left this note pinned to their hero's box: 'Hello Dessie. This is from two of your fans and admirers. Good luck for the Cheltenham Gold Cup and we assure you, even if you don't win, you'll still be the best there is! ... You are a true knight's charger, proud and graceful and full of guts, stamina and speed. You are a truly wonderful horse and we love you.'

Despite his stunning looks and brilliant performances on the turf, Dessie doesn't have Arab blood or even a particularly distinguished lineage. His grandmother was a hack hunter bought for a paltry £175 and his mother, point-to-point Flower Child, and sire Desert Mirage, a flat racer, have achieved little. It would seem, therefore, that Dessie owes his talent to nobody but his wonderful self.

---

In 1986 researchers at Kew Gardens revealed that bees navigate to pollen-bearing flowers by homing in on miniature 'landing lights'. Using electron microscopes, the researchers discovered that the leaves and petals of these plants have thousands of tiny 'optical cells' which act as reflectors and project light into the bees' eyes.

---

# Micky

In 1983 Christine Harrison's pet chihuahua, Percy, was killed by a car. Her father, Bill, dug a two foot hole, buried the unfortunate animal, then led his weeping daughter inside. Neither paid any attention to Micky, Bill's dog and Percy's arch-enemy, who remained in intense contemplation of the grave.

Seven hours later Bill was disturbed by a frantic scuffling and whining. Opening the back door to investigate he was horrified to see the muddy sack in which he'd buried Percy strewn across the garden path. Even worse was the sight of Micky just a few feet away hovering over Percy's 'corpse' in a frenzy of agitation. The gruesome notions that sprang to his mind vanished when he realized Micky was licking the chihuahua's face and nuzzling his mouth in a canine attempt at the kiss of life. Staring in disbelief Bill witnessed a resurrection miracle. Percy's limp body twitched, then he moved his head and whimpered weakly.

When the chihuahua's body had been retrieved from under the car there had been no doubt in anybody's mind that he was quite dead. Only Micky possessed the psychic sensibility to detect a faint spark of life still unextinguished. Micky was named Pet of the Year by the animal charity Pro-dog.

> In 1967 the entire population of a tiny island off the west coast of Ireland was evacuated by the Eire government. The only creature left behind was a small donkey, later given the apt name of Islander. Islander's lonely existence lasted for eighteen years. He survived on a diet of seaweed and grass and very occasionally, when a fisherman visited, his hooves were trimmed. He was eventually rescued and taken to a Devon sanctuary to end his days in comfort and – most importantly – in loving company.

# Ginger

Ginger was a very particular sort of cat. She didn't miaow when she wanted to be let in, she leapt up and knocked loudly on the door. Using this method she regularly got her owners, Mr and Mrs Ball of Southport, Lancs, out of bed in the early hours of the morning.

Ginger didn't only knock on her own door, however. She often played her own version of the children's game 'ring the bell and run away' when she took a stroll down her street. On one occasion she rapped smartly on the door of a neighbour to whose house Mrs Ball had gone visiting – her dinner time was approaching and she decided her mistress had been away too long.

Something of a despot, Ginger ruled the Ball household with an iron paw. She insisted on being fed full cream milk, baby food and the freshest of fish – anything else was scorned. She had definite views on a variety of things, most particularly Mrs Ball's singing which she absolutely hated. If her mistress dared burst into song, Ginger would give one of her spectacular leaps and smack her in the face with her paw. As Mrs Ball explained to the *Daily Mail* when they interviewed her with her pet in 1973: 'It's Ginger's way of saying, "that's enough", I suppose.'

Patti, an arthritic eleven-year-old English setter, was dearly beloved by her equally arthritic 74-year-old mistress. When the old lady died she proved that love by leaving her entire fortune of £250,000 to a Manchester doctor so he would provide Patti love, care and medical attention for the rest of her life.

# A Miraculous Cure

The ancient Greeks believed that dreams possessed the power to heal, entering the sleeping mind through what were called the Gates of Dreams. Patients would sleep in a special sanctuary and their dream images were analysed by priests and priestesses in search of divinely inspired clues. Sometimes these dreams contained details of herbal remedies, in others the person received a visit from a god, occasionally in animal form, and woke cured.

A modern example of a healing dream concerned a 64-year-old widower, George Edwards. He was admitted to London's Middlesex Hospital suffering from a brain tumour and with the left side of his body paralysed. One night he had a terrifying nightmare about his beloved corgi, Rufus, dreaming the dog was going to be put down. He woke with a violent start, describing 'a terrible jolt and big shock' which ran down his left arm and leg.

This was not, however, a prophetic dream of impending tragedy, it was the trigger for a miraculous cure. To the astonishment of doctors and nurses he began to make an immediate recovery and subsequent brain scans showed the malignancy had completely disappeared. Six days later George Edwards was discharged from hospital with a completely clean bill of health.

A farmer in Wisconsin, USA, fitted all his cows with specially designed bras. He claims that the support they give to the udders has resulted in a marked increase in the milk yield.

# Trepp

Trepp – short for Intrepid – is listed in the 1978 edition of the *Guinness Book of World Records* as 'the world's top police dog'.

Trained at the age of four to sniff out drugs, this 66 lb golden retriever showed his worth immediately. His first big success occurred after only two months of working life when he tracked down a massive 1 ½ tons of hashish stashed in the bulkheads of a vessel moored at Fort Lauderdale in the USA. Later, in 1975, he was on duty at Miami airport when a young girl hugging a doll disembarked from a plane. Her innocent look deceived everyone but Trepp. People stared in amazement as, barking loudly, he raced over and pulled the doll out of her arms. Subsequently examined by police, it was found to be stuffed full of cocaine.

Trepp's keen intelligence, acute sense of smell, and uncanny intuition combined to make him a phenomenon.

By 1979 he had been instrumental in securing over 100 arrests and recovering more than $63 million worth of drugs.

---

In 1987 the Cats Protection League (CPL) found homes for over 47,000 cats (feral and domesticated) and had just over 27,000 neutered. The league says that the number of cats in Britain who have gone feral after being abandoned is growing. There are literally thousands of colonies of them now in London. Hospital grounds and factory sites are the favourite breeding grounds.

# Inga and Raja
# Toto and Moto

Inga and Raja, two Indian elephants, had lived together in the zoo of Tajikistan's capital, Dushanbe, for twenty-seven happy years. But during the particularly severe winter of 1985 Inga contracted a lung infection and died. She was thirty years old and her death was a devastating blow to her devoted companion. Raja sank to his knees beside her, tears streaming from his eyes, and nobody could persuade him to move. Medical workers with a pulley contraption were called in to remove the body from the enclosure but Raja's anger drove them away.

Eventually, with difficulty and a lot of patience, the keepers succeeded in luring him into the sturdily built winter shed. It didn't hold him for long, however. Almost immediately he had battered his way out and returned to mount a twenty-four hour guard over his mate. This was clearly the mourning period the elephant needed to come to terms with his loss and when it was over he reverted to being his usual gentle self. He not only allowed the keepers back into the enclosure, he actually helped them lift Inga's body and carry it away.

A similarly touching story is told about two African elephants brought to Colchester zoo as babies. Toto and Moto had been friends for seventeen years when Moto died a sudden, and unexpected, death. For five hours grief-striken Toto guarded his body, caressing him obsessively with her trunk. When the keepers finally succeeded in removing him, Toto continued to caress the spot where Moto had lain.

When forester Joe Meacham found the orphaned foal he called Ginny she was too weak to walk and her chances of survival seemed zero. Nevertheless Joe carried her home and introduced her to his goat, Olive. Olive immediately took charge of the foal and within hours Ginny was suckling her hungrily. The strong mother/child bond that was established saved Ginny's life. She quickly began putting on weight and became a frisky, glossy-coated adolescent.

It was a bright day in March 1989 and 23-year-old Danish medical student Jan Ekstrom and his girlfriend, Utte, on holiday on the Isle of Skye, were enjoying a moment of romantic intimacy in the heather. Suddenly there was an ear-splitting shriek, a thunderous beating of six-foot wings and a massive white-tailed eagle swooped down on them. Jan, who rolled over just in time to see the terrifying bird with its beady eyes, sharp beak and long talons feet away from his head, leapt up with his jeans round his ankles. Screaming with terror, Utte snatched up her panties, grabbed Jan's arm and they ran off as fast as their trembling legs would carry them. The white-tailed eagle died out in Britain in 1900 but was reintroduced from Scandinavia in 1975. There are more than 100 of them in the Highlands and Hebrides now.

In March 1989 Kath and Vernon Dillurs were married in their home at Saarbrücken in West Germany. The unusual thing about the ceremony was that it was performed by Kath's Alsatian dog! Jules was ordained by a mail-order ministry and, according to Kath, is the first ever canine curate and entitled to perform all official ceremonies.

# The Custer Wolf

In 1915 a renegade wolf started a six-year reign of terror through ten counties around Custer, South Dakota, USA. The Custer Wolf, as people everywhere called him, would slaughter as many as thirty sheep or ten steers in a night, and his habit of mutilating a cow to get at the unborn calf made him particularly hated.

In one two-month period his trail covered a staggering 600 miles and his apparent invincibility elevated him to almost mythical status. The rabies epidemic of 1916, for example, killed many thousands of wild animals but left the Custer Wolf unscathed and as active as ever. Scores of experienced bounty hunters set out to track him down but failed consistently.

In March 1920, however, an enterprising man called H P Williams had the idea of luring the wily creature into the open by putting the scent of a female wolf on his boots. The tables were turned. Now it was the Custer Wolf who began tracking the hunter and he even tunnelled 50 ft underground to prepare a den for his phantom mate. When Williams finally succeeded in killing him he discovered that the wolf who had terrorized so many for so long was, in fact, rather small and insignificant looking.

The extraordinary story of this bloodthirsty, resourceful animal is told by Roger Caras in *The Custer Wolf*.

# Koko

Koko, a 230 lb gorilla, is probably the most famous of all the great apes who, from the mid-sixties, have been taught to communicate using the standard American Sign Language for the Deaf.

Her teacher, Dr Francine 'Penny' Patterson of Stanford University, California, taught her to use words ranging from airplane, belly button and lollipop to morally loaded words like steal, bite, lie and hurt. Her training began at the age of one and she built up a vocabulary of over 1,000 signs, 500 of which she uses regularly. Dr Patterson started by teaching her basic signs like 'eat' and 'drink', taking her hand and moulding it repeatedly into the shape of the sign. Koko learned quickly and was soon putting signs together to make sentences and giving them new meaning. On one occasion she expressed her passion for Coca Cola by signing the word 'coke', then putting her arms into the cradling position for love.

Koko has also shown her kinship to humans in the way she spontaneously began using language to lie, joke or give vent to her scorn. She was only five when she first tried to lie her way out of trouble. Having jumped on a sink and torn it away from its fittings, she tried to put the blame on Dr Patterson's assistant by signing, 'Kate bad there'. Another time she snatched up a red crayon and began chewing it. When Dr Patterson noticed and signalled crossly, 'You're not chewing that, are you?' Koko hurriedly

A grey-headed albatross chick on its nest.
*Oxford Scientific Films – Ben Osborne*

Time for a snooze . . . A female African lion, fast asleep.
*Oxford Scientific Films – Jack Dermid*

A lowland gorilla relaxes in the sun.
*Oxford Scientific Films – M Ansterman*

made the sign for lip and began rubbing the crayon across her lips pretending she was just applying lipstick. On yet another occasion she poked a hole through an insect screen with a chopstick and, on being rebuked, stuck it in her mouth and signed defiantly that she was only 'smoking'.

Her rich and imaginative vocabulary of insults include: 'dirty toilet devil', 'bad gorilla nut', and 'rotten bird'. She can use a camera, loves going for rides in a car and is fascinated by the telephone, which she dials at random for the delight of hearing a voice at the other end. Once she got through to the operator, who worriedly traced the call back because she thought she was talking to either a dying man or a 'heavy breather'.

Dr Patterson has given Koko a human intelligence test and calculates her IQ at 95 – only slightly lower than a normal human child.

---

On St David's Day (1 March) 1986 two ducks on a farm in Dyfed, Wales, started laying black eggs. By May they had laid a total of thirty-six ranging in colour from dirty grey to pitch black. Nobody was able to explain the mystery.

The black woodpecker of North America can eat 900 beetle larvae or 1,000 ants at a single mealtime. A European green woodpecker has an even more voracious appetite and eats 2,000 ants at a single mealtime. To find food the woodpecker hammers wood at the rate of fifteen or sixteen times a second – nearly twice as fast as a machine gun – and its head movement reaches a speed of 1,300 miles per hour. The bird's beak and brain are very well cushioned and its neck muscles ensure the head and beak are always in an absolutely straight line. If, while hammering, the woodpecker's head were to twist even slightly, the force of its pecking would tear its brain out.

For three days a rogue squirrel terrorized a quiet suburb of La Puente in California. During that time it bit four women, charged a fireman and held a pit bull terrier at bay. The rodent was finally killed after a wild ten minute chase involving fire and police officers, a sheriff's deputy and an animal control officer.

# Indigestible Curiosities

In 1979, the *Daily Star* reported the strange case of a fifteen-year-old Turkish girl who had suffered mysterious stomach pains and violent headaches for five years. During that time Yeter Yildirim changed from a sweet-natured, happy farmgirl into a moody, unapproachable individual. Folk remedies consistently failed to allieviate her symptoms and eventually her despairing family took her to a hospital in Ankara. There she was X-rayed and her problem at last became clear. Poor Yeter had three water snakes slightly thicker than string and a foot in length inhabiting her intestines. The doctors' theory was that she must have swallowed them as eggs while drinking from a stream aged ten; since then they had continued to grow inside her.

A 25-year-old Syrian woman, Khadija el Reefi, was even more unlucky. When she was rushed to hospital in 1982 with severe abdominal pains, a six-foot snake was found inside her. The Syrian daily *Al Baath* said that the snake 'cheeped' like a chicken when it was hungry and the noise was loud enough for Khadija and people nearby to hear.

For variety, however, one of the most amazing – and revolting – stories of this kind has to be that of Marianne Fisher. This 24-year-old girl was rushed to hospital in 1811 and was kept there for a whole year. During this time she discharged one frog, three small crayfishes, fifty-two leeches and eight worms. They had been in her body since she'd drunk marsh water the previous year.

Siri is a fourteen-year-old Asian elephant of New York's Syracuse Zoo who began spontaneously using a pebble to scratch marks and images on the concrete floor of her enclosure. Her keeper noticed and began supplying her with graphic materials and her artistic scope developed rapidly. It was subsequently discovered that all captive Asian elephants spontaneously mark their territories.

# Rogan

In 1971 a lady called Mrs Bailey went to the Cats Protection League in London and chose an endearing marmalade kitten to take home. She named him Rogan and for ten years he was her valued, if undistinguished, pet. Then in 1981 he won the ITV's Star Cat of the Year prize sponsored by a pet-food company, receiving a cheque for £1,000 and an avalanche of publicity.

Rogan's rise to celebrity status prompted his proud owner to set up a company called Star Cat Products, producing life-sized fake-fur Rogan lookalikes, T-shirts and feeding bowls emblazoned with his image. This venture was not a commercial success, however, and was soon eclipsed by the emergence of his true talent – psychic healing.

Rogan's singular gift was discovered after a woman spent half an hour with him on her lap in the back of a parked car and came out with her nervous breakdown cured. Word soon got round and people flocked to seek Rogan's help. Afflictions as diverse as slipped discs and fading vision were cured after a session of 'laying on of paws'. The cat would sit on the mountain of letters he received and, going into a psychic trance, effect instant relief to people suffering from a whole variety of complaints. He also cured a fellow feline, Smudgie, suffering from a form of moggie anorexia, Key-Gaskell syndrome. As Smudgie lived some distance away, Mrs Bailey sent a few combings from Rogan's coat which, once sniffed, sent Smudgie rushing to his bowl for his first proper meal in months.

This success encouraged Mrs Bailey to send combings of Rogan's fur to sufferers all over the world, achieving miraculous results. Rogan was featured in newspapers and magazines and his fame grew. A Californian radio station interviewed Mrs Bailey and invited her to take her amazing cat on a US tour. A Japanese film crew made a documentary about him, treating Rogan with such deference that they walked backwards out of his presence.

Rogan died in 1986 and Mrs Bailey sat down to write his biography, simply entitled *Rogan*, and published by Arcturus Press. Although she had vowed never to get another cat, when Mrs Bailey heard Rogan's voice urging her to pay a visit to the Cat Rescue Centre she obeyed. There she found herself guided to a cat who put his front paws on her face, instantly curing her chronic pyorrhoea. She immediately understood Rogan's design. Gus, as she named the new cat, was to be the medium through which Rogan would continue his healing from the other side.

Julie and Dick Morrow were terrified when in February 1989 they were woken by a violent crash from the room below, followed by the sound of voices. Julie dialled 999 from the bedside phone and within minutes two policemen were ringing the front door while another two nipped round to cover the back. It was only then that Dick dared venture out of the bedroom. When he peered over the stairs, however, he discovered that the 'burglars' were none other than the budgie, Bobby. Bobby had managed to knock his cage over (hence the crash) and then started squawking his head off (hence the 'voices').

# Brett The Wonder-Dog

A wind-swept mountain top in the heart of Snowdonia is the final resting place of a fourteen-year-old Alsatian called Brett. A slate erected in 1974 bears the simple inscription, 'He Mastered Them All'.

Brett was trained as a guard dog and during his eventful life was honoured with more than a dozen bravery awards and commendations. His first, from the RSPCA, was for heroically fighting his way down a Yorkshire mine shaft to rescue two terriers trapped behind tons of fallen earth. It took six attempts before he was able to locate them. He also called the attention of rescuers to blowholes in the snow which resulted in the recovery of a buried sheep. The whole area was then searched and fifteen more sheep were dug out.

Brett had been taught extreme gentleness; he could carry balloons or eggs in his mouth without damaging them. It was an ability he found useful on various occasions; like the time he rescued a small girl from drowning by delicately gripping her bikini strap in his huge teeth and hauling her to safety; or when he plucked a kitten from a log adrift in a lake and swam with it in this mouth to the shore.

By profession a guard dog, for three years Brett guarded the mighty Clywedge dam in Radnorshire against attacks from Welsh Nationalists. His courage was legendary and he lost an inch off his right ear when he tackled thieves wielding bicycle chains who were breaking into a shop. He'd also been trained to drop by parachute and earned himself a place in history when he became the first dog to leap from a helicopter in pursuit of a criminal. The last two years of this wonderful animal's life were spent conscientiously guarding a bus depot.

The houseboat community of San Francisco is driven mad every summer by a noise described as 'like an electric razor noise, only ten or fifteen times louder.' After eleven years of suffering the noise – which starts around 8 pm and goes on all night – it was finally identified as the mating call of the Singing Toadfish. The male of the species attracts the female by emitting a rasping drone from muscles surrounding the swim bladder. The drone has a frequency of between 50 and 130 herz and has been measured at 40 decibels.

# Krause

Mules, bred from male donkeys and female horses, have always been thought to be sterile. Then in July 1984 a mule called Krause mated with a donkey called Chester, resulting in the birth of a foal named Blue Moon. The event was so extraordinary that blood tests were immediately taken to ascertain whether mother and daughter were bona fide mules. The results confirmed that they were. Horses have sixty-four chromosomes, donkeys sixty-two and mules sixty-three. Both Krause and Blue Moon had the required sixty-three chromosomes.

Although experts claimed that the Nebraska wonder mule was the first documented case of mule fertility, the Burlington *Free Press* carried an article claiming there had been at least six previous documented cases of mules foaling, although in each instance they were bred by stallions and not donkeys.

A US congressman was so excited by the news of Blue Moon's birth he urged Krause's owners, Mr and Mrs Silvesters, to support his motion to make 28 October Mule Appreciation Day.

> Major Adrian Coles (rtd) fell in love with hedgehogs after rescuing one that had fallen down a cattle-grid near his home in Ludlow, Shropshire. He went on to found the British Hedgehog Protection Society, boasting a membership of over 5,000, and his 6 acre garden now has more hedgehogs per square acre than any other part of Britain. The Society receives letters from all over the world, including Japan, and they are often addressed simply to 'Major Hedgehog, England'.

# Michael Jackson and Bubbles

Six-year-old Bubbles is not only Michael Jackson's pet, he's also his best friend. This playful chimpanzee shares Jackson's super-star lifestyle, eating with him, lounging by his pool at the Santa Ynez ranch in California, and travelling around the world with him dressed in beautifully designed, custom-made outfits.

The eccentric singer has arranged to have his body frozen when he dies in the hope that science will have progressed sufficiently to bring him back to life sometime in the future. He has also written into his will that, if he should go first, when Bubbles' time comes he wants him frozen and placed next to him. Jackson's devotion to the chimpanzee is such that he cannot bear the thought of any life – even a resurrected one in the twenty-first century – without him.

> For thirteen years bounty hunters in South Dakota tried to catch an outlaw wolf known as Three Toes. During the animal's renegade career it is said to have destroyed $50,000 worth of livestock. A government hunter finally succeeded in capturing the beast in 1925.

# Sabre

There's a filling station in Burton Agnes, North Yorkshire that is guarded by an Alsatian called Sabre. He belongs to Tony Cooper and no amount of money could induce him to part with the dog because he knows he's priceless.

It was a freezing January night in 1984 when two youths broke into the station with the intention of committing a robbery. Sabre was sleeping in an outbuilding but he heard the noise and was immediately alert. With a snarling bark he launched himself at the intruders, undeterred by the vicious kicks their heavy boots aimed at his flanks. It was obvious the dog was not going to be easily frightened off and they soon realized they were in bad trouble. Spotting a length of two-inch iron bar lying nearby, one of the youths made a dive for it and cracked Sabre over the head. The blow left Sabre dazed and bleeding profusely but his only concern was to defend his master's property. A horrific fight ensued. The Alsatian charged the youths again and again while they kicked him and repeatedly smashed him over the head with the iron bar. Blood ran into his eyes and mouth and splattered all over his assailants' clothing. His legs buckled, his bark became a rasping croak and yet he still refused to give up. As he marshalled strength for another desperate lunge, the iron bar came down one last time and shattered his skull. Sabre collapsed on the ground and the two young thugs made a hasty getaway leaving the dog for dead.

The noise finally woke Tony Cooper, asleep in his house next door. He followed the trail of blood until he found Sabre huddled in a limp broken heap by a fence. His coat was drenched with blood and his skull had been smashed like an eggshell. Gently Tony gathered him up in his arms, convinced for one terrible moment that the animal had stopped breathing. Miraculously, however, Sabre was alive – if only just. The vet did all he could but ultimately it was the dog's pluck and resolute determination that pulled him through.

Sabre became an overnight hero and during the long months of his painful convalescence, letters and get-well cards arrived, not only from Britain, but from all over the world. He was also awarded the RSPCA's highest tribute, their Animal Plaque for Intelligence and Courage. Sadly Sabre will carry the scars of his exceptional heroism and devotion for the rest of his life. He has lost the sight of one eye and is deaf in his left ear. His head still looks handsome but beneath the fur are the sharp ridges left by the three fractures inflicted by that iron bar.

In April 1986 Yerba, a six-year-old German shepherd police dog, was awarded a posthumous medal for 'services to humanity' from the Canine Defence League. Yerba, who died when he was repeatedly shot by two armed robbers, continued to battle with them to the very last. His heroism delayed their getaway and enabled police to move in and make the arrest. Yerba's handler, PC Coxon, said that at least four people owed their life to the brave dog.

In 1949 a cat called Rusty followed its owner from Boston, Massachusetts, to Chicago, Illinois – a distance of 950 miles – in eighty-three days. To keep up such an extraordinary pace of more than 100 miles a day, it's assumed Rusty must have hitched lifts in passing trucks or trains. Rusty's achievement still stands as America's fastest reunion between cat and owner.

# Plastered Pigs

In 1778 Parson Woodforde made these entries in his diary:

April 15 ... We breakfasted, dined, supped and slept again at home. Brewed a vessel of strong Beer today. My two large Piggs by drinking some Beer grounds taken out of one of my Barrels today, got so amazingly drunk by it, that they were not able to stand and appeared like dead things almost, and so remained all night from dinner time today. I never saw Piggs so drunk in my life ...

April 16 ... My 2 Piggs are still unable to walk yet, but they are better than yesterday. They tumble about the yard and can by no means stand at all steady yet. In the afternoon my 2 Piggs were tolerably sober.

# Ballyregan Bob

Ballyregan Bob is the fastest greyhound in the history of the world. Retired in 1987 at the age of four, the 70 lb canine racing machine stands 27 in with a glossy speckled coat the colouring of a tiger – dark brindle as it's called in the sport. The last race he lost was in April 1985 and he went on to win thirty-one successive races, becoming the only dog to get under forty seconds over 7,000 yards.

He sleeps on a heated bed of shredded newspaper, breakfasts on cornflakes, milk, eggs and a spoonful of honey and has two security guards watching his kennel night and day. His main lunchtime feed comprises two pounds of meat cooked in a stew with onions, carrots, cabbage and pearl barley, plus a few vitamin pills. His main treat and passion are KitKat chocolate bars.

His owner, retired engineer Cliff Kevern, twice turned down £100,000 offers for him and during Ballyregan Bob's racing career the possibility of someone trying to steal him was taken very seriously. The doors on the kennel block where he lived were protected by burglar alarms and there were no name plates or numbers on the individual kennels. Routes to race tracks and the cars used were changed frequently. After retirement he was put out to stud, earning £500 a time covering bitches. He was expected to cover two a week for six years.

His trainer Bob Curtis retired around the same time, but he continued to handle him because the dog meant so much to him. 'It'd break my heart to lose touch completely,' he told the *Evening Standard* when it interviewed him. 'Bob's like a kid to me. I never had children. He knows me and I talk to him. People think I'm bloody potty like ... but you've probably got to be a bit crackers to spend a lifetime doing this.'

In July 1985 Taiwan farmer, Liu Ming-hui, was badly injured in a road accident. His life was saved by his intelligent prize pig who ran off to fetch help and led the rescuers back to the deserted spot where his master lay unconscious.

# Sparkie

In 1954 Mattie Williams, an English teacher from Newcastle-upon-Tyne, bought a six-week-old cock budgerigar from a local pet shop and called him Sparkie. She had never owned a bird before but the rapport between them was immediate and in just three weeks she had taught him to say 'pretty Sparkie'. The schoolteacher was impressed to find her new pet such a bright and willing pupil, although, at that point, she had no inkling of the extent of his potential.

After learning those two simple words there was no holding Sparkie back. He added to his vocabulary every day, not only with words he'd been taught, but with any words or phrases he overheard. Nine months later with a vocabulary of 300 words and 156 phrases, Sparkie's elocutionary skills were nothing less than phenomenal and, hearing that the BBC were organizing a budgie-talking competition, Mrs Williams decided to enter him. There were 2,768 feathered hopefuls prattling their hearts out, but Sparkie outshone them all.

The success made him an overnight celebrity. He was immediately signed up to star in a series of TV commercials advertising bird-seed, and shortly afterwards cut a record on which he explained the ins-and-outs of teaching budgies to speak. The single didn't make the top ten – but it did sell over 20,000 copies! During his eight year career as an avian celebrity, Sparkie mastered a total of 531 words, 383 sentences and 8 nursery rhymes. After he died in 1962, Mrs Williams claimed that his last words had been, 'I love you mamma'.

His heartbroken mistress had his stuffed body mounted on his perch and – together with a recording of his voice – donated him to the Hancocks Museum in Newcastle.

When 150 elephants broke into an illegal still in West Bengal and drank large quantities of the moonshine liquor, the consequences were disastrous. They proceeded to go on a rampage that killed five people, injured twelve others, demolished seven concrete buildings, twenty huts and several acres of corn. The story was reported in the *San Franciscan Chronicle* on 20 July 1974.

# Hachiko

Shibya is one of Tokyo's busiest commuter railway stations. Prominently placed in the tiled forecourt stands a statue of Hachiko, Japan's most famous canine. Hachiko's master, Dr Elizabura Ueno, taught at the Imperial University and every morning the small sturdy dog accompanied him to catch the train into Tokyo. And every evening, at the appointed time, he returned to welcome him home again.

One sad day in 1925, however, Dr Ueno had a heart

attack at work and died. That evening Hachiko arrived at the station as usual – but his wait was in vain. Eventually he trotted off, returning the following evening and the evening after that. The little Akita dog never gave up hope that Dr Ueno would come home and, no matter what the weather, he continued to meet his master's train every evening for nine long years.

It wasn't long before the small solitary figure sitting alert and expectant on the platform became a familiar sight to all the commuters. At first he was fed by a local milkman, but soon everybody was giving him tasty titbits and showering him with affection. Hachiko came to represent all the qualities most highly valued by the Japanese, especially those of loyalty and endurance.

To commemorate the 50th anniversary of Hachiko's death, another Akita dog called White Treasure was made honorary station master for the day. Together with his human counterpart, White Treasure made the rounds of ticket barriers, platforms, and the travel centre. The inspection finished in the station forecourt, man and dog stood in respectful silence in front of the statue of the famous and honoured Hachiko.

---

A polar bear's hairs are completely transparent, the fur appearing white because visible light reflects from the rough inner surface of each hollow hair. The hairs, however, are designed to trap ultraviolet light and the radiation is conducted along the hair to the skin. This summertime energy supplement provides up to a quarter of the bear's needs.

*Chalicodoma pluto*, or 'king bee' as the Indonesians call it, measures 1¾ in and is the largest bee in the world. It was first reported in 1859 by RA Wallace who sent a specimen to the British Museum from the North Moluccas. Thought to be extinct for over a century, two were recently discovered alive and well on Hamaher Island by biologist, Adam Messer. The insects were gathering tree resin with their curious, plier-like mandibles.

In September 1985 the *Jakarta Post* reported the presence of large flesh-eating catfish in the rivers of the Mâcon area of France. They are said to measure up to two metres, weigh around 60 kg and are not only decimating the populations of bream, pike, carp, tench, crayfish, freshwater mussels, but are even having a go at waterfowl and ducklings. In some areas there have been rumours of swimming children being attacked.

# Sewer Crocodiles

Horror stories of baby crocodiles that are flushed down toilets and grow into great sewer-dwelling albinos are usually taken with more than just a pinch of salt. In March 1984, however, municipal workers in the ancient sewers below Paris discovered a young crocodile wandering aimlessly through the dark dank tunnels which have since been turned into a tourist attraction. The 2 ft 7 in reptile – which was definitely a little pallid – was thought to be about four years old. The ten firemen who were called to the scene managed to overpower the creature and transport it, bound and gagged, to the Jardin des Plantes. It now enjoys a comfortable – and more fragrant – life in a vivarium.

A year earlier nineteen-year-old Barry Robertson was strolling down a street in Cains, Queensland, when a 3ft 9in crocodile suddenly burst out of a gutter drainhole and lunged at him. The incident was witnessed by a passing taxi driver who slammed on the brakes and ran to Barry's aid. The reptile had clamped its jaws around Barry's leg and it was only by virtue of his sturdy cowboy boots that he escaped a very nasty injury.

# Yeti Photographed

In March 1986 Anthony Wooldridge, a researcher for the Central Electricity Generating Board in the Greater Manchester area, embarked on a solo 200-mile charity run in the Garhwal Himalaya of North India.

He was trekking at about 3800 metres on his way to Hemkund when he discovered that a recent wet snow avalanche extended right across his intended route. When he moved to a better spot to survey the obstacle and assess the risks of proceeding, he noticed a set of large tracks leading across the slope, behind and beyond a spindly shrub. Standing behind the shrub was a large erect figure about 2 metres tall and conforming to descriptions of the large legendary man-like or ape-like creature alleged to inhabit the Himalayan mountains – in other words the famous yeti or Abominable Snowman.

He described the moment thus: 'It was difficult to restrain my excitement as I came to the realization that the only animal I could think of which remotely resembled this one in front of me was the yeti. My scepticism about the creature's existence was overturned by this all-too-real creature, standing with its legs apart, apparently looking down the slope with its right shoulder towards me. Its head was large and squarish and the whole of its body appeared to be covered in dark hair, although the upper arm was slightly lighter in colour. The creature was amazingly motionless although the bush vibrated once or twice, and

The following letter appeared in April 1989 in London's *Evening Standard*; 'Cull pigeons? Certainly not. They are doing a better job than London Transport cleaning up the tube. Six pigeons boarded my train at Edgware Road the other day and walked around the compartment picking up pieces of fast food discarded by passengers. When the train arrived at the next stop, Paddington, all six lined up by the doors and hopped on to the platform together, presumably to catch the return train and rejoin their families.'

In 1968 American oil heiress, Eleanor Ritchley, left her 161 dogs $4.3 million. It is the largest bequest to dogs ever made.

On 7 January 1989, dark clouds gathered over outback Queensland in Australia, accompanied by a loud drumming sort of noise. Mrs Debra Degan looked out over the fields of the family farm near Brisbane expecting a typical late summer hail storm. Her amazement knew no bounds, however, when what she saw tumbling out of the sky was not hail but sardines! Scientists speculate that a violent updraft scooped the fish into the air, carried them thirty miles inland, and dropped them as 'rain'.

When American Gene Alba and his girlfriend split up in 1983 he decided to seek a new soul mate at the dog pound. He immediately fell for a mongrel with big melting eyes, took him home and called him Mutley. From that moment on the two were inseparable. Mutely rode pillion on Gene's motorbike, went snow skiing with him and, most amazing of all, became his scuba diving companion. To make this possible, Gene had a diving suit especially adapted for him.

Guy the Gorilla, one of London Zoo's past stars with a bronze statue erected to his memory, never showed the slightest interest in any of the female gorillas who at various times shared his cage. Although several keepers suspected the hulking primate was homosexual, all that is known for certain is that he died a virgin.

when I moved back down to lower ground, it appeared to have changed the position of its head, now looking directly at me.'

Wooldridge then took a number of photographs from an estimated range of 150 metres, unaware at the time that nobody had ever photographed a yeti before.

Predictably the photographs created a lot of interest back in Britain. John Hunt, leader of the successful 1953 Mount Everest Expedition had twice seen yeti tracks himself and was fascinated by the images. His main concern, however, was that nothing should be done to prejudice the animal's wellbeing and, particularly, that no attempt should be made to capture it. Zoologist Dr Desmond Morris gave four possible explanations of the figure in the photographs: an unknown species of bear or monkey, a Sadhu – holy man or hermit – or the fabled yeti. Dr Brian Bertrand, curator of mammals at London Zoo, said he could suggest no known mammal which could be confused with the animal in the photographs and, in particular, was sure it couldn't be a bear.

Professor John Napier, the anatomist and a leading authority on primates said the photographs had reversed his previous scepticism. 'There is a remote possibility that the figure is that of a Sadhu and therefore *Homo sapiens*' he's quoted as saying, 'but in my view it is not a human in the general sense of the word, although it may belong to the genus *Homo*. The creature cannot be anything but a yeti – it is neither a langur (it has no long tail), nor a bear (legs too long, no muzzle) – unless we wish to invent a mysterious animal that is being mistaken for another mysterious animal!'

In the final analysis Wooldridge's photographs have not solved the great mystery. What they have done, however, is rekindle serious interest among experts in the yeti's existence.

A tortoiseshell cat belonging to Pamela Fletcher, a farmer's wife of Bradwell, Derbyshire, climbed a 15 ft tree to give birth to three kittens in an abandoned magpie's nest.

# Incitatus

Caligula Gaius Caesar (AD 37–71), was the most grotesque figure ever to serve as Emperor of the Roman Empire. He was cruel, tyrannical, deranged and most of his subjects wished him dead. Fanatical about horse racing, Caligula treated few humans, if any, with as much respect and generosity as he did his favourite horse.

Incitatus (fast speeding) started life with the not so grand name of Porcellus (little pig) but, correctly in this instance, the Emperor considered the name unworthy of the magnificent stallion and changed it. Incitatus ran like greased lightning and never lost his august master a race. In return he received not only Caligula's veneration, but the opulent lifestyle of a prince.

His magnificent villa was run by a retinue of obedient slaves. It boasted a huge marble bedroom with big bed of sweet-smelling straw that was changed daily, an ivory manger and solid gold drinking bucket. The superb frescoes decorating the walls and ceilings were all painted by famous artists. On the days prior to the big races that took place at Circus Maximus Caligula sent his soldiers around Rome ordering the populace to keep silent so that Incitatus's sleep would not be disturbed. His victories were celebrated by Caligula and select dignitaries with orgies of eating and drinking at the stallion's house. The horse was always offered the same food as everyone else, although he repeatedly refused it until he got what he wanted – a very ordinary bowl of barley.

On one of these festive occasions he suddenly reared up, sending one of his horseshoes hurtling across the room. It smashed into an alabaster cup that had belonged to Julius

Caesar and spilled wine everywhere. Caligula, who was very superstitious and lived in constant terror of assassination, saw this as an extremely ominous sign. And well it might have been because not long afterwards he was murdered.

The Emperor first honoured Incitatus by making him a Citizen, then a Senator. At the time of his death Caligula was said to have been thinking of promoting the horse to the position of Consul, one of two annually elected magistrates who jointly exercised the highest authority in the republic.

---

On 26 August 1985 the Beaumont *Enterprise* reported that the wife of Sioux Indian, Benny Left Hand, had discovered a gold nugget weighing about an ounce in a chicken she'd killed and cut up. The nugget's value was estimated at over $500. When the story got out, there was a continual stream of people trying to steal the Left Hands' chickens.

---

# Cut Throat

Cut Throat was the prize pigeon of Bill Shillaw, of Wentwork, South Yorks. Early in 1984 he took the bird to some woods a couple of miles from his house and released it. As Cut Throat rose into the air a volley of gunshot suddenly rang out and the pigeon plummeted out of the sky. Bill stared in horror, certain his favourite bird was dead. Too upset to try and find its body, he returned home. He was totally amazed, therefore, when two days later he saw Cut Throat dragging himself slowly up the garden path. The exhausted pigeon, who trailed a wing shattered by shotgun pellets, had walked across fields, through woods and across a busy main road to find his way home.

# Rats

In 1978 a stray mongrel wandered into an Ulster barracks. Although he wasn't much to look at, he had the mongrel's sharp, street-wise intelligence and cocky charm. He was an immediate success with all the soldiers who began giving him regular meals and called him Rats.

In return for their kindness, Rats decided to stick around and join the ranks. Over the next two years the dog was a regular member of army foot and air patrols tackling IRA terrorists in Ulster's perilous border country. In the many dangerous skirmishes he was subsequently involved in, Rats never once faltered in his devotion to duty or showed any fear.

But in 1980 his health began to fail and it was decided that the time had come for Rats to retire. He was flown to barracks in Pirbright, Surrey, where an officer presented him with a medal for his loyalty and courage. After the solemn ceremony, during which a band played and Welsh Guards stood stiffly to attention, he flew off in another military plane for a retirement home 'somewhere in Kent'. The exact location was a closely guarded secret to protect Rats (and his keepers) from terrorist reprisals.

On the afternoon of 5 March 1984 a huge swarm of bees descended on the Mission District of San Francisco, USA. The threatening dark cloud of an estimated 10,000 bees hovered in the air for several hours before heading back to the building where they'd made a giant nest.

When Lattie, a Labrador retriever of Wareham, Mass, USA, stopped eating her worried owner took her to a vet. On examining her the vet found a strange lump in her stomach which an X-ray revealed to be a 10 in long, 14 oz wrench. After removing the object, the vet said it had been in Lattie's stomach for at least a month.

# Tall Story?

On 10 July 1985 an extremely curious occurrence was reported in the following American newspapers: the Boston *Globe*, the Houston *Chronicle*, the San Franciscan *Chronicle*, the San Diego *Union*, the Pawtuxet Valley *Daily Times* and the Seattle *Times*. It happened just before dawn on 6 July 1985 when Greg and Stephanie McKay were asleep in their tent at a site in Pierce County, about five miles off Highway 410, near Greenwater in Washington State.

In a statement made later to the Pierce County Sheriff's office, the couple alleged that they were rudely awoken by the arrival of an 8 ft, bear-like creature with a curly brown coat and an overpowering odour. The enormous creature loomed over them and in a high-pitched, inhuman voice' demanded to know if they had permission to be there. They were so frightened it took a moment before either of them were able to speak. When they found their voices and told him they did have permission, the bear got very irate. It ordered them to get off the property immediately and, while they were frantically gathering up their possessions, began pelting them with stones.

The Greenwater fire department was speedily dispatched to the scene. They checked the camp area thoroughly but reported that the only tracks they could find were those of a large dog. The McKays wanted the search extended to a wider area but the Sheriff's office refused. In a statement to the press Deputy Bob Hoffman dismissed the talking bear as a product of the couple's over-active imagination.

This is what the eighteenth century Swedish botanist had to say about reptiles and amphibians in his famous work, *Systema Natura*: 'These foul and loathsome animals are distinguished by a heart with a single ventricle and a single auricle, doubtful lungs and a double penis. Most amphibia are abhorrent because of their cold bodies, pale colour, cartilaginous skeletons, filthy skin, fierce aspect, calculating eye, offensive smell, harsh voice, squalid habitation, and terrible venom; and so their creator has not exerted his powers to create many of them.'

# Simon and Sally

In 1963 the giant tanker *Torrey Canyon* was wrecked off the Cornish coast and oil swamped the sea and beaches for miles around. During that period Ken Jones and his wife, Mary, worked day and night to rescue the seals and birds who'd been caught up in the slick.

One of the victims was a four-week-old seal pup suffering so badly from lung congestion that it was clear he'd never be able to return to the wild. Ken took him home, built a pool for him, and called him Simon. Simon formed a passionate attachment to Ken, jumping up at him like a dog and trying to knock his cap off. And if Ken had to go away for a couple of days, he'd sulk for a week.

Not long afterwards another badly damaged seal pup was washed up on a nearby shore. There was a violent storm that night and Ken had to be lowered down the rain-lashed cliff on a rope to reach her. She was badly cut, blind, and so terrified that she attacked anything that moved. Ken brought her back to the house and put her in the pool with Simon. But Sally, as they'd decided to call her, didn't attack the other pup. They nuzzled each other inquisitively and an immediate friendship was born. Somehow Simon knew at once that Sally was blind. He became her eyes, never leaving her, leading her everywhere and nudging her towards food.

But the following year Simon's health deteriorated rapidly. He was unable to eat and his lungs weakened to such an extent he had to fight for every breath. During one particularly bad attack, Ken jumped into the pool fully dressed to hold the gasping seal's head above the water.

On the day he finally died, Ken and Mary carefully laid his body by the side of the pool. Barking with distress, Sally heaved herself out of the water and lay on top of him. She refused to move and tried to fight them off when they attempted to take her companion away. Despite her efforts, however, they eventually succeeded in removing his body for burial. Sally was heartbroken and remained motionless on the spot where Simon had lain. She refused food or comfort and, after five days of terrible grief, she died.

Twelve-year-old Linda Heslop and her sister Karen were very excited about their school holiday in America. But when the postman delivered their passports and visas along with an unsolicited chocolate sample, their pet Yorkie ate them up. Frantic efforts to get new documents issued in time failed and they missed the flight. They were so disappointed that, despite Yorkie's whimpering appeals for forgiveness, they refused to talk to him or give him any affection. Eventually, however, the sisters relented because, in Linda's words, 'We just love him too much.'

For 200 years swallows have been making a 5,000 mile flight from Argentina to arrive at the Mission San Juan Capistrano in California on 19 March. They arrive just as the sun is about to cross the Equator on its way north to signal the official start of spring.

# Radar

Radar, a German shepherd, suffered such chronic distemper as a puppy he was never expected to survive. He was rescued from pitiful neglect by Dorothy Steves, then living in Brazil with her husband, who nursed him back to health with determined love and care.

He grew into a beautiful and intelligent dog whose amusing and spirited performances at dog obedience classes led to him being written into a top Brazilian TV series and becoming a superstar. He received sack-loads of fan mail and the following article in the *Times* of Brazil was typical of the press he received: 'Radar is a dog, but people tend to forget this. Perhaps it is because of his remarkable intelligence and undoglike behaviour that prompts people to hold conversations with him. He is certainly treated like a human being by Dorothy, his proud owner and trainer, and even the house servants say "excuse me" to him when they pass.'

When Dorothy decided to return to England Radar naturally went with her. His departure from Brazil was an occasion of national sorrow and 20,000 tearful fans turned up to wave him goodbye. Despite his star status, however, he was treated just like any other dog by British immigration officials. He was collected in a special van and packed off to do a six-month quarantine stint in adequate, but not luxurious, kennels.

He resumed his showbiz life the moment he was released, though, wooing viewers on the prestigious David

Frost Show by nonchalantly picking up the receiver of a ringing telephone as he sauntered in.

Although the British never gave him the same adulation he received from the emotional Brazilians, he nevertheless acquired a considerable following when he teamed up with PC Snow in the long-running TV serial, *Softly Softly*. Radar's charmed life continued until he died, aged twelve and a half.

> The animal charity Zoo Check says twelve out of the twenty polar bears in British and Irish zoos show signs of mental illness. Born to prowl the vast Arctic wastes, the animals are driven mad by confinement to their concrete pits. A tragic example of this is Misha who shares a 360 square metre pit at Bristol Zoo with Nina. Every day for over ten years he's paced his enclosure, rolling his head, clicking his tongue and maniacally swaying from side to side.

# Troy

It was a bleak January day in 1981 and seven-year-old Allan, at home recovering from chicken-pox, was feeling bored. After consistent nagging, he eventually persuaded his stepfather, Ron, to take him for a walk to the Kings Mill reservoir near their home in Mansfield, Nottinghamshire. Tagging along with them was the family pet, an eight-month-old German Rottweiler called Troy.

While Ron strolled on ahead, Allen decided to explore one of the jetties that jut out over the water. Skipping over the slippery, moss-covered duckboards Allan's wellington-clad feet lost their footing. The next instant he had plunged over the edge, through the thin ice, into the freezing water.

Unable to swim, and with his pullover, scarf and anorak immediately waterlogged, Allan was swiftly dragged under.

The more he struggled the more he was carried away from the jetty and death seemed only minutes away. Ron was alerted by his terrified screams. He knew he'd never be able to reach the child in time and instinctively slipped Troy's lead, yelling: 'Fetch!'

The powerful animal – eight stone of solid muscle – cleaved through the water and reached the boy just as he was going under again. He grabbed Allan's collar with his jaws, ensured the boy had got a good grip on his own collar, then turned and swam back to shore with him. Troy had been bought for £150. But to Allan and his family he's worth his weight in gold.

---

The Atlanta-based Orkin Pest Control Company has named Miami as the top termite-threatened city in America. They calculate that in 1988 alone the insects consumed the equivalent of 452 three-bedroomed houses with two bathrooms and a two-car garage.

# Bad Omens

In 1985 a group of scientists on a field study trip in the autonomous region of Xinjiang reported seeing a collection of 'red boats and a mass of seaweed' in the remote Lake Hanas. A closer investigation with binoculars, however, revealed that the 'boats' were in fact enormous red fish. The sighting was considered alarming news by the local Mongolian population. The last time the big fish had made an appearance in the lake was in the 1930s and shortly afterwards a major earthquake had devasted the region.

Xiang Ligai, an associate professor of the Xinjiang University, arrived to study them. On 23 July 1985 he spent ten hours making detailed notes and sketches of the fishes' head, spiny rays and tail fin. With the information he'd gathered, Xiang Ligai was able to identify the red monsters as a huge species of salmon known to China as *hucho taimen*. *Hucho taimen* are usually found in the rivers of Heilongjiang, China's northernmost province, and generally measure about 6 ft 6 in. In Lake Hanas, however, some of them had reached a staggering 33 feet in length.

A few weeks after Professor Ligai's identification the superstition that the presence of giant fish in the lake was a bad omen was, sadly, proved correct. An earthquake rocked the province and eighty people died.

> The cat who features in the opening credits for *Coronation Street* got the part when it casually wandered on the set one day. After being filmed the cool feline strolled off and was never seen again.

# Annone – The Pope's Elephant

In the beginning of March 1513 a ship flying under the flag of the King of Portugal and commanded by the famous navigator, Tristan da Cunha, put down anchor at Porto Ercole, Italy. Like Noah's Arc, a procession of assorted animals sent as gifts to Pope Leone I from the king were led off. The most spectacular of all these animals was an Indian elephant, later named Annone, accompanied by his Indian handler and Saracen groom. When the lengthy disembarkation was completed seventy animals and forty-three men, led by the king's envoy Tristan da Cunha, set off for Rome. News of the extraordinary caravan spread like wildfire and crowds flocked to gape along the whole of the seventy mile route. But it was the magnificent Annone, stumbling a little over the unfamiliar stony ground, who drew the most oohs and aahs.

The procession arrived at the city gates on 11 March – a day earlier than expected – and were lodged in the villa of an important cardinal to prepare for their official entry the next day. Annone was quartered in the gardens and within minutes of their arrival hordes of people were scaling the walls or trying to prise cracks in the bricks to get a look at him.

The following morning, Tristan da Cunha and the other Portuguese nobles attired themselves in sumptuous silks and velvets while the horses and mules were decked out with ornate drapes. Annone, star of the occasion, was washed clean of the dust accumulated during the long journey and covered with a caparison embroidered with the Portuguese crest in gold. On top of this was secured a silver structure in the shape of a tower containing jewels and other precious gifts for the Pope. With the Indian handler sitting on his neck and the Saracen groom walking beside him, Annone led the procession from Piazza del Popolo through the streets of Rome.

As soon as they were sighted at the Vatican, Pope Leone I and his court took the secret passage leading to Castel Sant'Angelo and mounted the Borgia tower. Papal gunners fired the guns, sounded the pipes and beat the drums in welcome. The excitement of the surging crowds became even more frenzied. On reaching the foot of the tower, Annone knelt three times and, lifting his trunk to the Pope, trumpeted majestically. Leone I and his court were as enchanted by the elephant as the rest of the city and from that moment on Annone was the undisputed darling of Rome.

Annone took up residence in the Vatican city. The common people were allowed in to view him every Sunday when he was escorted by none other than the Pope's Master of Chamber, Giovanni Battista Branconio. During these occasions Annone would show off his dancing skills and entertain the crowds with a variety of tricks. There's an amusing story of the part he played in a joke designed to cut an insufferable poet called Baraballo down to size.

Having a very inflated sense of his own importance, Baraballo immediately agreed when it was suggested he should be crowned in the Campidoglio as the great Roman poet Petrarch had once been. On the appointed day he was seated on a throne on Annone's back to be carried in pomp to the place of the ceremony. Half way there, however, the elephant gave a sudden loud trumpet, shook his huge body, and sent Baraballo tumbling to the ground. Bruised, covered with dust and, above all, humiliated, the poet fled along the banks of the Tiber and was never seen again.

But in 1516 Annone fell ill. The Pope instructed his own doctors to treat him and the diagnosis was that he was suffering from angina. These learned men prescribed the standard treatment for anybody – human or animal – suffering from the complaint at that time: powerful laxatives reinforced with 500 grams of gold powder. Not surprisingly Annone got worse and, on 15 June of the same year, he died.

Pope Leone was deeply saddened. He himself composed Annone's epitaph and commissioned the great painter Raphael to paint the elephant's life-sized portrait. Sadly the painting and epitaph have been lost but drawings of Annone made by Raphael and Giulio Romano are still conserved in the Vatican.

For many years a North Chingford road sweeper had the company of a cheerful mongrel called Spot when he went on his rounds. After he retired Spot, who couldn't adjust to sitting around the house all day, tried to attach himself to his replacement. For some reason this arrangement didn't work out and Spot was unhappy until he managed to make friends with the postman. After that he accompanied him delivering letters all over the neighbourhood.

When Indra the elephant's trainer was sentenced to a year in jail for drunken driving she pined for him so intensely she couldn't eat. No morsel, however delicious, could tempt her and her weight plummeted by a dangerous 500 lbs. The German circus who owned her sought the emergency intervention of the court. After deliberation it was agreed that 31-year-old Alfons Koller was to spend two hours a day with his devoted charge. This had the immediate effect of making Indra eat again but she was still desperately unhappy and listless the rest of the time he was away. There was another meeting and this time the court decided that Alfons should be allowed to spend the whole day with his elephant, returning to prison only at night. This arrangement suited Indra perfectly and she was soon thriving again.

# Bede

Sixty-three-year-old Father Louis Heston was very attached to his four-year-old English setter, Bede, and Bede was very attached to him. Which made it all the more distressing when the dog suddenly disappeared during a summer holiday in Cornwall in 1976. Father Heston searched for him everywhere but Bede seemed to have disappeared into thin air. Deeply saddened, Father Heston resigned himself to never seeing his pet again and returned home to Essex.

Then six months later someone told him they'd seen a dog very similar to Bede only seven miles away. Father Heston lost no time in rushing to the spot. When he got there he found that the dog not only looked like Bede – it was him! A very emotional reunion followed. The dog was footsore, very bedraggled and beside himself with joy.

During his incredible 300 mile journey home, Bede had struggled across moors, trekked through dozens of towns and villages and braved the traffic in London's hard and dangerous streets. Father Heston was full of admiration for his dog's brave spirit and determination. So were the Kennel Club of Great Britain – they awarded him their 1977 award for Most Courageous Dog.

Jilly Cooper's dog, Barbara, has an awesome and unconventional appetite. She has consumed forty stuffed toys, three watch straps, Mozart's Prague Symphony, the peak of Jilly's ratting cap, the funnel of her hair dryer, four pairs of her shoes and two pairs of her husband's, and has chewed her basket down to the base. In her book *Intelligent and Loyal*, she tells the story of another great, if more normal, eater. Sandy, after wolfing down his own hearty dinner at home, would make a nightly visit to a neighbour who always cooked him an omelette and gave him a large lump of cheese.

# Jackie

When Albert Marr joined a South African regiment to fight in World War I, he took his pet chacma baboon to the battlefields of France with him. Jackie was immediately adopted as regimental mascot, given his own rations and paybook and kitted out in a cut-down uniform.

Brave, intelligent and very friendly, Jackie raised everyone's spirits during those grim, unhappy times. Although this in itself was more than enough to make him a welcome presence, Jackie was also able to put his acute hearing to invaluable use as the regiment's guard. The moment he picked up sounds of an enemy approach the baboon ran down the length of the trench, tugging at coat tails and giving his comrades extra time to marshal a defence.

Early in 1916 Albert Marr was hit by a sniper's bullet.

Two nine-month-old Highland calves.
*Oxford Scientific Films – Alastair Shay*

Two love birds, doing what comes naturally.
*Oxford Scientific Films – Steve Littlewood*

A brown bear, disturbed while fishing.
*Oxford Scientific Films – David C Fritts*

Conditions in the trenches were very bad, especially in winter: knee-deep in freezing mud and appallingly insanitary. All during the long wait for medical assistance Jackie squatted at his master's side, continually licking the wound in an attempt to keep it clean and free from infection.

By April that year the regiment had succeeded in advancing to Flanders. The fighting was fierce and during one heavy bombardment both Jackie and Marr were wounded. The baboon's injuries were particularly severe. His right leg had been so badly shattered by shrapnel that the doctor had no choice but to amputate. By this time Jackie had proved himself a courageous and loyal soldier. His services to his regiment were acknowledged with a medal and the promotion to rank of corporal.

In 1919, riding on a captured German tank, Corporal Jackie took part in the Lord Mayor's triumphant Victory Parade through the streets of London and shortly after returned to South Africa with Albert Marr. He had little time to enjoy his retirement on his master's farm, however. He died in 1921, two short years later.

The belief that an aphrodisiac love potion can be extracted from the fins of dolphins has resulted in large numbers of these beautiful and intelligent creatures being killed by Japanese fishermen.

Kentucky Fried Cock is a fearsome man-hating cockerel. His method of attacking humans is to leap 6 ft in the air and fly at them with talons ready. He starts crowing at 2.30 am every morning (waking the entire neighbourhood), dislikes chicken feed and gorges himself on meat bones and chips. In March 1989 his owners Pat and Ray Kelly of Watchet, Somerset, decided they'd had as much as they could take and advertised for someone to take him off their hands.

Gregory Peck was a rogue budgie. He particularly enjoyed attacking the poor cat, stealing the rabbit's food and, above all, dive-bombing the family's dinner. On one occasion he didn't right himself in time, though, and finished floundering in a bowl of soup.

# Chance – The London Fireman's Dog

Thomas Tilling was a famous Victorian horse-master who took over the old Adam and Eve Stable Yard in Peckham and turned it into a horse-omnibus station. One autumn evening in 1882 he noticed a darkish brown, short-haired stray, a cross between a bull terrier and a mastiff, with a few other breeds thrown in too, nosing curiously around the yard. The dog approached Bruce, one of the bus-horses, sniffed his hoofs and said hello with a bark. The horse shook his head and neighed at him and a great friendship was born.

For the next six weeks the mongrel established himself at the station, seeing Bruce off to work in the morning and welcoming him back affectionately at night. Then one evening he went for a walk and didn't return. A fire had broken out in some offices off Fleet Street and the horse-drawn fire engine, Fire Queen, from the Chandos Street Fire Station was on the scene.

Fireman Dick Tozer had just rescued a clerk when the mongrel from Peckham suddenly appeared and rushed over to him. He was barking excitedly and making runs towards the doorway of the burning building. Dick immediately understood what the dog was trying to tell him – somebody was still trapped inside. He followed the mongrel who led him to a locked door which he started scratching frantically. Battering it down with his shoulder, Dick Tozer stumbled over a young girl who'd been overcome by fumes. He picked her up and rushed outside with the dog jumping and yapping about his heels.

The Prince of Wales, an enthusiastic amateur fireman, was present and had witnessed it all. When it was all over, he noticed the dog was trotting quietly behind the fire engine and, back at the Chandos Street station, he curled up on the straw beside the horses and went to sleep. 'Looks as if he's adopted you,' the Prince of Wales said to Dick Tozer. 'You should call him Chance. He arrived by chance.' And so it was that in 1882 Chance was officially adopted by the Chandos Street Fire Station. They gave him a collar with the inscription: 'Stop me not, but onward let me jog. For I am Chance, the London Fireman's dog.'

Shortly afterwards it was decided to retire the older of the two fire-horses, Bob, and a new bus-horse was purchased to replace him. On the day he arrived the fireman witnessed a touching reunion. The horse took one look at Chance and began tossing his head and pawing the ground, while the dog raced madly around in paroxysms of delight. The bus-horse, of course, was none other than Chance's friend, Bruce, from Peckham.

The following day the Chandos Street firemen were called out to a burning house in Seven Dials. It was Bruce's first fire and when he smelt smoke he began to rear up and whinny with fright. Because of this it was decided to push the fire engine the rest of the way and Bruce was the first horse to be unhitched. The moment he was free he bolted, ears back and eyes rolling. When Chance shot after him barking urgently, Bruce's panic subsided somewhat and he began to slow down. Chance was able to grab the end of the trailing rein in his teeth, pull Bruce's head round, and lead him back.

Chance was in every way a true fireman's dog. He could get through smoke faster than any fireman and he had a sixth sense when it came to finding an injured person. He would be up the fire-escape even before Dick Tozer and could break into a window with the hind part of his body and enter backwards – a method he'd devised himself.

He proved himself a hero many times over, including one occasion when water, rather than fire, was the danger. It happened on a foggy autumn day when a small boy fell into the river by a warehouse off Lower Thames Street in London. Alerted by the alarmed cries of a small crowd of people on the quayside, he dived into the water and seized the child's jacket in his mouth as he came spluttering and choking to the surface. He managed to keep his head above water until rescuers arrived in a rowing boat.

Then one tragic day, while doing his duty, part of a wall in a burning building collapsed on him. Dick Tozer carried the fatally injured dog back to the station and made him as comfortable as possible in a basket in the corner of the watch-room. Heartbroken, he squatted next to him hoping to bring the dog a measure of comfort by his presence. Suddenly the fire alarm clanged and Chance tried to struggle up to answer its call as he'd done so many times in the past. His glazed eyes fixed on Tozer's face, he gave a feeble bark, then collapsed. The life of a brave, dauntless and intelligent fire-fighter was over.

In October 1988 the world held its breath as rescuers fought for three weeks to rescue three grey whales from their prison in the Alaskan ice. The joint life-saving mission by Americans and Russians cost a total of $2 million.

George Papayiannis is the designer of up-market residences for dogs. A Tudor-style timbered affair with a wood tiled roof of Canadian shingles and an elegant black and white tiled floor was on sale at Harrods for £4,000. Papayiannis can also offer a Georgian-style residence, a 7 ft wide villa and a pretty summer house.

In 1939 a peasant woman disappeared for twenty-seven days in a forest area of central China frequented by elusive ape-men creatures known as the 'wild men of Hupeh'. On her return she revealed that a group of them had kidnapped her but denied that sexual relations had taken place. Nine months later, however, she gave birth to a simian-looking baby who survived to adulthood, dying in 1960. In 1980 his bones were dug up and examined by Chinese scientists who confirmed they had the characteristics of an ape and a human.

# Butterscotch

A palomino gelding by the name of Butterscotch has a very unusual talent which earned him an entry in the *Guinness Book of Pet Records*. He is the only horse in the entire world who can drive a car.

Owned by Dr Dorothy Megallon of Kentucky, USA, Butterscotch motors around in his very own, specially converted, flame-red 1960 Lincoln Continental. The car has a drawbridge ramp for the horse to enter and works by a series of rubber control hoses. Butterscotch starts the engine by pulling the starter lever, pulls the gearshift into 'drive', steps on the enormous accelerator and then steers by turning the padded steering-wheel with his muzzle. To sound the horn – which gives him considerable enjoyment – he bites on a central lever. When he wants to stop he simply presses the brake pedal. Butterscotch knows the difference between left, right and straight and he obeys the rules of road safety by always wearing his outsized safety belt.

In March 1989 Cathy Hague found the family's pet hamster lying in his cage stiff as a board and apparently dead. Knowing how upset her three sons would be, she was determined to try and resuscitate the animal. As he was too small for the kiss of life, she sprinkled him with water and put him under the grill. It was an unconventional approach but it worked. Within minutes his tiny legs started moving and he was soon up and about. But the People's Dispensary for Sick Animals were not overly impressed. As a spokesman said, 'We don't recommend putting hamsters under the grill.'

# Slippery Thieves

Salmon fishermen working off the Northumberland coast were driven to despair by the wily poaching activities of grey seals from the Farne Islands. The success of their plundering reached such a peak that by 1973 several of the fishermen had quit their boats for jobs ashore. The seals, venturing as far south as Tees, would shadow the boats, wait for the nets to be cast and, when they were full enough, move in for a feast. Their cunning and intelligence was quite uncanny. After a while they actually began 'shepherding' manoeuvres, driving the fish into the nets in order to have richer pickings.

Somnuemk Promsong, a market trader of Bangkok, Thailand, is selling a bizzare cocktail from his city centre stall. He mixes a double measure of whisky with the fresh blood of a King Cobra to achieve an oriental version of our own Bloody Mary. Somnuemk claims it is an excellent tonic for both body and soul.

# Afra

In March 1974 eight-year-old Romana Strasser was happily playing ball in the farmyard of her home at Aurolzmuenster, Upper Austria. She was engrossed in throwing it into the air and catching it when her father's 700 lb prize pedigree boar suddenly knocked down the gate of his sty and charged her.

It was an horrific attack. The animal butted Romana to the ground, buried his vicious tusks in her hip and slit the flesh up to her shoulder. Her piercing screams of terror and agony brought the family's five-year-old Alsatian, Afra, racing to the scene. He leapt onto the deranged creature's back and, seizing its ear, forced it to lift its head and release the child.

Romana underwent four operations and endured a long, painful convalescence before she recovered. But if it hadn't been for Afra's brave intervention, she would have died.

When the cell door clanked shut behind him on the first night of an eighteen-month jail sentence for fraud, Alberto Pagini burst into tears. He was inconsolable until a young rat scampered across the floor and nuzzled his shoes. It was the start of a remarkable friendship and the only thing that made Alberto's stay in Rome's Regina Coeli prison bearable. On his release he took his friend for a celebration drink in a local bar. When his back was turned, however, the manager rushed over and smashed the rodent on the head mistaking him for one of the many against which he regularly waged war. Heartbroken Alberto instructed his lawyer to sue and had Roland stuffed.

# Mike

While out on a walk Clint Rowe came across a neglected, snaggle-coated Scottish border collie tied up outside an abandoned ranch house. There was nothing immediately special about him except that he had one blue eye and one brown, a feature Clint found so appealing he took him home. He soon discovered, however, that the dog had more than just charming mismatched eyes; he could do the most amazing tricks – including climbing a rope ladder with a bucket in his mouth. There and then Clint decided that Mike, as he now called him, was star material and set about launching his career.

He had only done a couple of minor TV commercials when he got his first big break: the star canine role in the Disney film *Down and Out in Beverly Hills*, playing the neurotic pet of an equally neurotic couple (Bette Midler and Richard Dreyfus).

When the movie came out in early 1986, seven-year-old Mike found himself an overnight star with a lifestyle to match. He was jetted first class to New York for the movie premier and booked into one of the best rooms in the classy Ritz-Carlton Hotel. Suddenly he was the dog everybody wanted to meet. Newspapers fought for exclusive interviews, prestigious TV chat shows clamoured for his participation and 'Good Morning America' gave him their prime spot.

Not a week went by when he didn't have to fly out from California to fulfil an engagement somewhere or other. A TV crew took him on a shopping expedition along Beverly Hills' Rodeo Drive, one of the most exclusive streets in the world, where Mike bought himself Gucci accessories and left his paw print immortalized in cement on the sidewalk. Every time he stepped out of a plane or limousine he was mobbed by adoring fans who tried to run their eager fingers through his (now) silky coat. He was inundated with offers for movies, TV series, etc, and Disney wanted to place him under exclusive contract. Clint turned them all down, though. After consulting with his shrewd, screwy-eyed prodigy, he stated sagely, 'Mike and I agree that we don't want to rush into anything.'

In January 1984 *The Times* newspaper reported the reappearance in Australia of the supposedly extinct Tasmanian Tiger, otherwise known as the Tasmanian Wolf and *Thylacinus Cynocephalus*. The news so excited Ted Turner, American TV mogul and yachting enthusiast, that he offered a $100,000 reward for a positive sighting of the beast. The ranger who'd actually seen the animal however, kept it a secret for eighteen months because he feared the shy creature would be harassed. The last Tasmanian Tiger was sighted in 1936.

The first living creature to orbit earth was an 11 lb Samoyed husky bitch called Laika. She was launched into space on 3 November 1957, in Sputnik II, just one month after the historic Sputnik I. In those pioneering years, however, re-entry and recovery were not yet possible. When the oxygen supply ran out after ten days, poor Laika died.

On 4 October 1959, a female rhinoceros was elected to the municipal council of Sao Paolo, Brazil, by a landslide 50,000 votes. The animal's victory – a protest against Brazil's corrupt politics, high cost of living and food shortages – merited a front page story in the *New York Times*. It wasn't the first time Brazil had shown preference for a non-human candidate, however. In 1954 a goat was elected to the city council of Jaboata, Pernambuco. It's name was Smelly.

# Sarah and Washoe –
# The First
# Communicators

When Samuel Pepys was introduced to a baboon in August 1661, he was so struck by its similarity to man that he felt sure it 'already understood much English' and wondered if it might not be taught to speak or make signs? More than 300 years were to pass before, in the 1960's, scientists began seeking an answer to that very question.

Sarah, a chimpanzee, was the first ape to learn to communicate using a visual language. She was taught by an American psychologist, David Premack, who devised a series of coloured plastic chips of different shapes to represent words. The shape of the symbol was abstract and gave no clue to the meaning of the word. For example, the symbol for 'apple' might be a blue triangle, the symbol for 'banana' a red square. Sarah quickly learned that by picking up the red square, for example, she would be rewarded with a banana. When she had acquired sufficient vocabulary, she progressed to arranging the plastic chips on a magnetized board to form sentences like, 'Give Sarah apple.' She was also able to read commands and carry them out. When tested with the sentence, 'Sarah place apple pail banana dish', Sarah duly placed an apple in the bucket and the banana in the dish.

She went on to learn characteristics such as *colour* and *shape*, the concept of *same* or *different*, the *interrogative* and the *negative*. In a complex experiment, Sarah also demonstrated she had properly understood the conditional *'if then'*. Using the plastic symbols Sarah was told that if she ate an apple (which she didn't much like), she would get chocolate. But if she took a banana (which she much preferred), she would not get chocolate. As chocolate was something Sarah was particularly partial to, she intelligently chose the apple. The experiment with Sarah was a landmark achievement in animal/human communication.

A second major breakthrough occurred in 1966 when Beatrice and Allen Gardner, husband-and-wife psychologists at the University of Nevada, began training an eight-month-old female chimp called Washoe to use the sign language for the deaf, Ameslan. The Gardners raised Washoe almost as if she were their own child and either they or their student assistants spent between twelve and sixteen hours with her every day. If two or more people were with Washoe, they were required to use sign language not only with the chimpanzee but also with each other. Laughter and sounds were permitted, but the spoken word was banned. Within a year Washoe was associating gestures with specific words or activities. By 1967 she was also making rudimentary sentences. If thirsty, for example, she would make the symbol for 'give me' and then the thumb in mouth, fingers drawn into a fist which meant 'drink'. If she wanted specifically lemonade then she first made the sign for 'sweet' – a quick touching of her tongue with her fingertips. Her other signals included putting her hand on top of her head for 'hat', cradling her arms for 'baby', spreading her hands palm upwards for 'book', and patting the underside of her chin to mean 'dirty'. Washoe also coined the poetic 'drink-fruit' for watermelon and 'water-bird' meaning a swan. After she was moved to the Institute for Primate Studies in Oklahoma, Washoe met

Available from Harrods for pampered dogs: a Dri-Dog bag in soft towelling to pop the pet in after wet, muddy walks; a jogging suit available in three sizes with the exclusive 'H' monogrammed on the side; a Sherlock Holmes outfit, designed by an American dogswear couturier, complete with tartan collar, cape and deerstalker hat.

The most common names for dogs used to be Rover, Spot and Lassie. Top favourites now are Ben, Sam and Sophie.

A *cattalo* is a cross between a bison and a cow. A *mule* is a cross between a mare and a donkey. A *hinny* has a stallion father and a she-ass mother. A *tigon* is sired by a tiger and mothered by a lion. A *ligor* is sired by a lion and mothered by a tiger. Hybrids are usually infertile.

In the late forties and fifties, three million people a year visited London Zoo, with 83,000 packing in on Easter Sunday in 1953. Today the situation is very different. In 1988 attendance had dropped to 1.3 million visitors a year and on a winter day in 1989 the zoo would be lucky to attract 350 people.

Danzas is officially listed in the *Guinness Book of Records* as the world's tallest dog. He is a Great Dane 40½ in high – or 6 ft 8½ in standing on his hind legs – weighs 16 st and has a 44 in chest. He consumes 4 lb of meat and two pints of milk a day, supplemented by biscuits and the occasional cake.

Booboo the Owl was taken on by an RAF airbase to scare birds away from aircraft. Unfortunately neither Booboo nor his service career ever got off the ground. The fact was that this supposedly fearless bird of prey was agoraphobic and so terrified of heights that he stubbornly refused to fly. The owl was given an honourable discharge and allowed to sit around the base all day.

other chimpanzees for the first time since she moved in with the Gardners in 1966. She gave them the unflattering name of 'black bugs'.

In 1979, after giving birth to babies who died, she adopted an eleven-month-old male chimpanzee and began teaching signs to him. After he'd thrown a tantrum, he kept signing 'hug' to her until she relented and gave him one. It was the first case of cultural transmission of language between species.

In August 1973 textile worker John Sutcliffe opened his front door to find a thin, exhausted ginger kitten on his doorstep. He picked the creature up hardly able to believe his eyes. It was the same kitten his wife had given their granddaughter as a present twenty five days earlier. The cat had walked more than 150 miles to find its way back to the home he'd been born in.

# Big Spot

Nola Schey and her husband Don share their home in Wisconsin, USA, with a huge 70 lb pig called Spot. He eats with them, cuddles up to watch television with them and is even allowed to share the marital bed. Mr and Mrs Schey insist that pigs are both intelligent and very clean. They don't have sweat glands and therefore never smell unless their human masters keep them in unhygienic dirty sites. Spot doesn't have that problem, he's very pampered. He's given a regular, twice-weekly scrub in a scented bath, is served his favourite pizza topped with pepperoni and mushrooms, and scoffs gallons of strawberry and vanilla ice-cream. His preferred viewing is Hill Street Blues and Lassie but he also grunts his approval at the video the Scheys made of him when he was an appealing piglet.

Dr Roger Mugford, the famous animal psychologist who treats the Queen's corgies, thinks that pigs generally get bad press and agrees that they can make marvellous pets. 'They love affection and will follow those they love around with as much devotion as a puppy,' he says. 'They are also incredibly loyal and crave body contact with people. They adore being caressed and scratched behind the ear.'

Pigs are also the only mammals to share man's love of a good booze-up. Their tipple? The rotting, fermenting windfalls found in apple orchards.

> Sam the mongrel was not highly regarded by his owners. He was just another mutt as far as they were concerned and moving from Montrose in Colorado to Santee, California, USA, they off-loaded him onto a neighbour. But Sam had a lesson to teach them about love, devotion and nobility of heart. He tracked them down over 840 miles across four states and arrived weak with hunger and exhaustion on their doorstep. Chastened, the couple welcomed him back and, at last getting the care and affection he deserved, Sam made a quick recovery.

# Adam and The Dolphins

One minute seventeen-year-old Adam Maguire was happily riding the big waves off the north coast of Sydney, the next he was plunged into a living nightmare.

It happened in February 1989 at the height of the Australian summer. The teenager was treading water waiting for the arrival of a big roller when a 12-foot shark suddenly cleaved through the water, bit a huge chunk out of the surf board, then sunk its teeth into Adam's right side. Helpless friends watched in horror as Adam fought for his life. But he was no match for the monster predator who, frenzied by the taste of his blood, was moving in for the kill.

It was at that moment a school of dolphins, who'd somehow become aware of his danger, arrived on the scene. Thrashing wildly, they began swimming in ever decreasing circles until they were able to isolate the shark and chase it back out to sea.

Adam was losing a great deal of blood but he managed to drag himself out of the water before collapsing on the beach. Shortly afterwards he was in hospital undergoing emergency surgery. His injuries were bad but, thanks to the intelligence and compassion of the dolphins, he lived to tell the tale.

---

More than 800,000 birds were ringed in Britain and Ireland in 1987. The oldest British ringed bird is a Manx shearwater, first ringed as a nestling on Copeland Island, Co. Down, on 21 August 1954 and retrapped at the same site thirty-three years later. More than twenty species reach back twenty years and in 1988 a tawny owl beat the species record by four years. The oldest known ringed wild bird in the world is believed to be the royal albatross. Several have been found which were ringed off in New Zealand before World War II.

---

# Judy

Judy, a thoroughbred English pointer born in Shanghai in 1937, lived through more adventures than most swash-bucklers. Fascinated by the sea she'd hung around several boats before being officially adopted as mascot by a British gunboat patrolling the Yangtze river in 1942. But Judy was to be very much more than just a mascot and pet. After taking part in a number of actions during the Malay-Singapore campaign – during which she showed her mettle by raising timely alarms of imminent attacks – the ship was bombed and the surviving crew took refuge on a small, uninhabited island on the route to Java. There was no fresh water and the men faced certain death until Judy discovered a fresh water spring near the seashore.

Shortly after Judy and her companions made their escape from the island in a commandeered Chinese fishing boat, they fell into enemy hands and were deported to a Japanese prisoner-of-war camp. The conditions were horrific, the guards were brutal and starving men risked death by raiding the Japanese rice stores.

During her two years there Judy proved her worth over and over again. She acted as a look-out and on one occasion, when suspicious Japanese guards arrived to search her hut, raced around the room with a human skull she'd dug up in her teeth. It was solely because of this wily performance that they failed to find the stolen rice hidden in a blanket.

Although Judy was friend and ally to all the men, it was here that she forged a special bond with RAF technician Frank Williams. They became so close that when it was decided to ship a number of prisoners to Singapore, Frank took the risk of smuggling Judy on board with him. They never reached their destination. During the voyage the boat was torpedoed and Frank was picked up by a Japanese tanker and taken to another camp. Judy seemed to have disappeared and he resigned himself to the fact she must have drowned. But Judy was very much alive and for many hours swam from man to man boosting their morale and giving them strength to stay afloat. Their relief when they were finally rescued was short-lived, however. All survivors, Judy included, were sent to Sumatra to work on the infamous 'death railway'.

The dog's instinct for imminent danger was uncanny and she used it time and time again to the benefit of her friends. Her spirit was indomitable and during that dreadful time it's said she even managed to produce a litter of puppies! Happily Frank and Judy were eventually reunited. When the war was over she went with him, first to

England, then to Tanzania where she died in 1950.

Judy is the only dog to have been officially registered as a prisoner-of-war.

> Between 1764 and 1767 the inhabitants of the Cévennes Mountains of south-central France were terrorized by a mysterious animal they called the Wild Beast of Gevaudan. The creature was said to be able to spring prodigious heights, use his tail like a club and had an overwhelmingly foul odour. He was variously thought to be a hyena, panther or rabid wolf.

# Misse

In 1877 Miss E Maier of Stuttgart wrote this charming description of her budgerigar:

'It was very tame, and at a call would fly to my shoulder or my hand. Then it learnt the trumpet notes of a pair of zebra finches and forgot the call of the robin. I therefore sent the finches away so that "Misse" – as I had named the parakeet – had no intercourse with other birds and soon it also forgot the robin trumpeting. How great was my astonishment and delight when one day it greeted me with the words "Come dear little Misse come" which it at first pronounced hesitatingly, but soon loudly and distinctly. I had always saluted it thus in the mornings, but without the intention of teaching it to speak. Not long afterwards it began to say also "Oh you dear little Misse, you little darling, come and give me a kiss". It is most charming to see it and hear it, when it plays with my finger, kissing it, then singing and trying to eat it. It flys away, returns and repeats these gambols countless times, during which it continually chatters the above words.'

William and Sandra Wood were asleep when in March 1989 a fire broke out in their mobile home in Venice, Florida, USA. The toxic fumes had already begun to take effect and their cat, Smokey, had to leap repeatedly on Sandra's stomach before he could waken her. William and Sandra escaped to safety. Little Smokey died.

# Nipper

In April 1985 a fire started in a large barn on Ansty Farm in Sussex. The blaze spread with such ferocity that farm workers were forced to abandon their attempts to rescue the 300 or so animals trapped inside. Only Nipper, the farm's five-year-old collie, refused to give up. Time and time again he plunged through the flames to shepherd terrified ewes, lambs, cows and calves to safety. It was the most extraordinary and moving performance. Choking on the poisonous fumes, his paws blistered and fur badly singed by the flames, Nipper battled tirelessly until he had single-handedly led all but nine animals out of the inferno.

He earned the eternal gratitude and respect of all the farm-hands and was awarded the animal world's VC: a plaque with an engraved dedication to his 'intelligence and courage'.

Flora Thompson fell off her pony while out riding in Northumberland in March 1989. For three hours she lay on a blizzard-swept hillside with a broken hip. Fortunately her Labrador, Dallas, had come out with her. With great care he covered her body with his and kept her warm until rescuers arrived.

# Kali

Kali, who lives at the Guilsborough Grange Bird and Pet Park near Northampton, is a mixture of collie, Labrador, Alsatian and a few other breeds too. But while she might not have much of a pedigree, she's the most gentle and loving mother. What makes Kali particularly special, however, is that she has never been in season or had a litter of her own.

Her supermum potential came to light in 1978 with the arrival at the Pet Park of two ten-day-old lion cubs. Kali took one look at the vulnerable babies and an extraordinary thing happened – her nipples began to swell up with milk. The miraculous surge wasn't just a trickle, either. Kali had enough to suckle the lion cubs until they were ready for solids. Since then the amazing mongrel has fostered two pumas, two arctic foxes and a leopard. On each occasion the same miracle has occurred. One look at the abandoned cub and her maternal milk flowed.

---

In 1987 a one-year-old cat hid in the back of a lorry travelling from Paris to Welwyn Garden City. The spokesman for truck owners MSAS Cargo International, of Bracknell, announced that the stowaway had been named Top Cat and said, 'He hitched a lift with us to start a new life in Britain and it's our duty to look after him.' But meanwhile a French newspaper, *Le Parisien*, renamed him Napoleon in his absence and started a campaign to have him sent home. MSAS was unperturbed. They footed the £400 six month quarantine fee and gave him a comfortable home in the company's headquarters when he came out. And in case the French had any plans to continue their battle, they let it be known they'd fight 'tooth and claw' to keep him.

# Alex The Parrot

For a long time it was widely believed that talking birds have no understanding of what they are saying and are merely mimicking. But in 1980 Dr Irene Pepperburg of Purdu University, Indiana, published a report that made the scientific world do some serious rethinking. In it she described her experiments with an African grey parrot called Alex whose use and understanding of spoken English far surpassed anything anyone had hitherto suspected.

The bird had proved a brilliant pupil, learning to ask for and refuse forty separate objects, mostly food and toys. The training sessions were carefully structured. With Alex watching attentively from his perch, Dr Pepperburg acted out short scenes with an assistant – one playing the instructor and the other playing the 'parrot' role. The instructor would hold up an object and ask the 'parrot' for the name. If the 'parrot' answered correctly there would be warm praise, if 'he' got it wrong there would be a sharp 'no' and a disapproving turning away of the head. Afterwards Alex would be quizzed to assess what he'd managed to take in.

The exciting discovery that Alex was capable of expressing an independent wish was made early on in the project.

After eating an apple, he spontaneously asked for a piece of paper and then began using it to clean out his beak. He later asked for a nail file and used it for the same purpose. There was also the occasion he requested a piece of cork, repeatedly refusing a well-pecked piece he was offered until he got the new bit he wanted. Alex also learned to distinguish between a square, triangle, oval and pentagon and identify colours such as blue, green, grey, yellow and rose.

It was the expression of an abstract emotion, however, that convinced Dr Pepperburg that parrots and other talking birds possess real intelligence and, like chimps, are capable of acquiring the rudiments of language-like behaviour. That memorable moment happened when Alex told Dr Pepperburg that he feels miserable when he moults.

In order to conform with the rigid breed standard rules, certain pedigree dogs are bred to exaggerate typical characteristics to the point of deformity. Pekinese are a tragic example, with some toy breeds so genetically tinkered with that the bitches are no longer able to whelp properly and have to be delivered by Caesarian section. They often suffer from cleft palates, chronic breathing problems (sometimes necessitating an operation to cut back their nasal cartilage), and have eye problems because a double set of eyelashes is considered a sign of great beauty. Each pedigree breed has its own list of potential breeding problems. The West Highland Whites are prone to eye and skin disease, Cavalier King Charles spaniels suffer disc and heart problems, many Dalmations are born deaf as a result of in-breeding, toy breeds suffer slipped kneecaps and large breeds like Labradors, Rottweilers, Dobermanns, Burmese Mountain Dogs and Great Danes have a tendency to suffer from spinal problems.

# Chip

Chip and his young master Nicholas Conner often went down to the beach near their Sussex home to play. They usually started off chasing each other up and down the sand followed by the collie's favourite game, fetch. This entailed Nicholas throwing a ball as far out to sea as he could and the dog tearing through the water to get it.

It was a blustery day on 14 April 1985 and Chip had already returned several times, dripping wet and tail wagging, with the ball in his mouth. The next time that Nicholas threw it, however, the dog ignored the ball and swam out a further 200 yards. Nicholas watched mystified as the dog raced towards a small object floundering in the choppy waves, busied himself with it for a few moments, then swam back to shore with something in his mouth. The 'something' turned out to be a seagull which had become so enmeshed in a fishing line it was unable to take flight.

Back on dry land he continued to show his concern, watching attentively while Nicholas carefully disentangled the seagull from the yards of line and barking with delight when it was eventually able to flap its wings and soar into the air.

The extraordinary aspect of the rescue was not only the mysterious way Chip had recognized the bird was in danger of drowning, but also that he cared sufficiently about a creature he had no natural affinity with to do something about it.

---

Fred is the name of a 7 ft long, 5 cwt sow. In February 1989 she escaped from her pen and rampaged for two and a half hours through gardens at Hedge End, Southampton before exhausted police finally managed to coax her back into her sty.

# Marocco

For many hundreds of years village fairs and town festivities included performing animals that supposedly possessed supernatural abilities, could communicate with people or were simply phenomenally intelligent. History records tales of talking dogs, wise pigs and even a goose who purportedly read minds. One of the most extraordinary of these animals, however, was the famous 'talking horse', Marocco, who belonged to a gentleman called John Bank.

Marocco thrilled crowds all over France in the late sixteenth century and was so famous in Elizabethan England that many writers, including Shakespeare, Ben Jonson and Sir Walter Raleigh, mentioned his accomplishments. This remarkable horse could dance, recognize colours and would bang a sliver-shod hoof to indicate the sum total of two hidden dice or to add up the coins that the admiring spectators put in his master's hand. Marocco's rare talents led to John Bank being suspected of witchcraft and sorcery.

In March 1987 a striped lamb was born on a farm in North End, Warwickshire. The lamb, thought to be a genetic freak, was aptly named Zebra.

This letter was sent to a woman's weekly magazine by Fay Lifschitz, of Hatch End, Middlesex: 'My neighbour's cat has a passion for water. While the dishes are soaking he will put his face in the suds, and will sit under the tap for hours with his mouth open and a daft expression on his face. My favourite story was when, during the course of Sunday lunch, my neighbour took the dishes into the kitchen and there was the cat curled up in a saucepan floating around in the sink!'

# Remus

Remus, an Alsatian police dog, was courageous and eager to please – but he just couldn't tell the cops from the robbers. In March 1989, in pursuit of a man who'd committed a particularly violent armed robbery, his handler slipped his collar and told him to 'go get 'im!'

Remus immediately sprang forward but, instead of going after the criminal, he made straight for Inspector David Cox who was leading the chase. It was a terrifying moment for the Leicester police officer when he turned to see a hurtling missile with snarling teeth and claws coming straight at him. He barely had time to put his right arm up to protect his face and head, when Remus's fangs fastened around the sleeve of his heavy top coat. It took a while for Remus's handler to persuade his triumphant dog to unclamp his jaws and allow a white and shaken David Cox to pick himself up from the ground.

Remus redeemed himself later, however, by sniffing out the robber from his hiding place. Inspector Cox showed he wasn't a man to bear grudges by giving him a glowing reference.

Thirty-nine-year-old Melvin Mantell has converted the 25 ft extension of his family's home into a reptile house. He keeps tree frogs, terrapins, newts, lizards, tortoises, African toads and two crocodiles. Oscar, a Caiman crocodile, is now fourteen years old and over 5 ft long. Tich, a dwarf African specimen, is ten and nearly 3 ft. Melvin lavishes time and affection on his pets despite getting nothing in return. 'They just sit there and wait to be fed,' he says mournfully. 'They don't distinguish me from anyone else who feeds them.'

Organized cat thieves supplying the cat fur market,
vivisectionists and people involved in illegal dog fights (the cats
are used as bait) have been particularly active in Eastbourne,
Worthing, Bridlington and Wrexham. And over a four-week
period in 1987 over 100 cats went missing in Lewisham and
Greenwich in South London. Particularly at risk are tortoiseshell, tabby and white cats.

# Raffles

Raffles, a mynah cock, was a phenomenal mimic who
became a fêted celebrity throughout the USA. The American explorer, Carveth Wells, plucked him from a nest in
Malaya while still a fledgling and became so fond of him
that he took him home.

Raffles' exceptional talent manifested early. He was
particularly good with *The Star Spangled Banner* and his
patriotic rendering was in great demand during the
troubled years after the outbreak of World War II.

As his fame grew he was often heard on the radio and
film producers vied with each other to sign him up. In one
year alone his personal appearances netted $15,000 and
Walt Disney was so impressed by him he threw a lunch
party in his honour.

Like other show-biz personalities, Raffles did his bit for
the war effort too. He travelled to hospitals all over the
United States, entertaining the wounded soldiers who'd
returned from battle grounds overseas. In recognition of
his unique contribution he was presented with the
prestigious Lavander Heart award in 1943.

Three years later Raffles died at the age of only eight,
mourned by Wells and his large following of grateful and
admiring fans.

# Queenie

Queenie was a police sniffer dog on duty at Harrods when an IRA bomb explosion killed and maimed scores of people shortly before Christmas in 1983.

Five minutes before the bomb went off the Alsatian clearly sensed something was going to happen. Whining and barking with anxiety she desperately tried to drag her handler, PC Gordon, away from the scene. Tragically he didn't heed her warning. Shortly afterwards he was one of the many lying in a pool of blood on the pavement, his right leg and all the fingers of his right hand torn off in the blast.

Queenie's injuries, however, were even more severe and the heroic dog had to be destroyed.

> In January 1989 a renegade band of twenty-two hamsters escaped from a pet shop at Maesteg, South Wales. The outlaws plundered a vegetable market before they were eventually rounded up.

# Gerry

When John Sullivan, the painter, was a small child his family had a pet Labrador named Gerry. He was intelligent, affectionate and playful and John loved him very much. But at the beginning of World War II the Government was recruiting dogs to fight alongside the troops in the battle against Hitler and John's father offered Gerry to do his bit. The parting was very sad for all the family and there was to be no reunion.

In April 1945 the Sullivans received the following letter which John has treasured all his life:

Any further communication on this subject should be addressed to:—

The Under-Secretary of State,
The War Office
(as opposite),
and the following number quoted.

BM/V&R/632/C
Your Reference...................................

P9/660

THE WAR OFFICE,
DROITWICH SPA,
WORCESTERSHIRE.

14th April 1945

Sir,

It is with great regret that I write to inform you that No.3055/8488 Newfoundland X Labrador dog "Gerry" has been killed in action whilst serving with the British Armed Forces in North West Europe.

I hope that the knowledge that this brave dog served our country well, will in some measure mitigate the regret occasioned by the news of his death.

I am directed to express our appreciation of your generosity in loaning "Gerry" for War Service and our whole-hearted sympathy in your sad loss.

It is hoped that on cessation of hostilities when materials are more plentiful, certificates of service will be issued to owners in respect of all War Dogs.

I am, Sir,
Your obedient Servant,

H. A. Clay
Major
for: Brigadier.
Director,
Army Veterinary & Remount Services.

J.E.Sullivan Esq.,
18 Ivorydown,
Downham, Bromley, Kent.

# Anna

Twenty-one-year-old Johnny Leonard, a petty thief and would-be bird-snatcher, had no idea what he was in for when he set his sights on a cockatoo called Anna. At first all went smoothly and according to plan. He threw a brick through the window of the Alaska Tropical Bird Shop in Anchorage, USA, plucked the white plumed bird from its perch and made off down a side alley.

Cockatoos are one-person birds, however, and Anna was outraged at being manhandled by the insolent stranger. Screeching and flapping her wings she suddenly flew at him like a malevolent Harpy, first clawing his face then chewing up his hands with the efficiency of a chain saw. Johnny's terrified scream brought Police Sergeant Mike Fullerton racing to the scene. He found the burglar bleeding profusely from deep wounds and still locked in mortal combat with the maddened bird.

Johnny was arrested and jailed under a $10,000 bond. Anna, on the other hand, suffered no more than a few ruffled feathers and became an overnight celebrity. She was unfazed by her new status and the steady stream of people who came daily to gawk at her at the pet shop received nothing more than a cold, steady stare.

---

The following epitaph appears on the gravestone of a dog named Fritz: 'Fritz. A German Sausage Dog. Killed crossing the road near Tonbridge. His front part crossed safely, his after end was hit by a Triumph motor cycle. Gott Straffe motorcyclists.'

Kysami Kinu, a Japanese Akita, did what many suffering contestants have probably wanted to do when he bit one of the judges at a dog show. He paid for his misdeed dearly, though – he was banned from dog shows for life.

Great apes belong to the primate family, a group that ranges from small monkey-like animals known as prosimians through monkeys and the great apes to *Homo sapiens*. Gorillas are the largest of all the primates alive today. Wild males in the mountains and lowlands of equatorial Africa frequently exceed 500 lbs in weight and, when they stand erect, are about 5 ft tall. Contrary to popular myths, field and laboratory investigations have established that great apes are both less aggressive and less sexually active than humans.

# Mary Tealby and The Battersea Dogs' Home

Mrs Mary Tealby was the estranged wife of a Hull timber merchant who lived with her retired clergyman brother in Islington. Her life was that of a typically respectable Victorian matron until, one summer afternoon in 1860, she visited Mrs Major in nearby Canonbury to take tea. On this occasion, instead of being shown into the drawing room, her friend hurried her down to the kitchen where a starving dog she'd rescued was lying comatose in front of the range. Mrs Tealby's heart was deeply touched by the pathetic heap of skin and bone and she immediately offered to help look after it. It was the start of what was to be a lifelong passion.

Over the next few days the two middle-aged women brought back more miserable, disease-ridden creatures to nurse with food, medication and loving care. It soon became clear, however, that two lone women were not going to be able to solve the problem of the countless starving strays roaming the streets of Dickens' London on their own. It was then Mrs Tealby began urging her initially reluctant brother to enlist the support of some of his influential friends. Her persistence resulted in the founding of the now world famous Battersea Dogs' Home.

The first committee meeting was held in the Pall Mall offices of the Royal Society for the Prevention of Cruelty to Animals and was chaired by the future fifth Marquess Townshend, who continued as Patron and President for the next twenty years.

Mary Tealby and her associates were all motivated by a love of animals and a deep concern for their welfare. They are the same sentiments that drive everyone involved with the Dogs' Home today and these lines by Byron appear at the beginning of every Annual Report:

> With eye upraised, his master's looks to scan
> The joy, the solace, and the aid of man;
> The rich man's guardian and the poor man's friend,
> The only creature faithful to the end.

Just after Christmas in 1982 the proprietor of an antique shop in Surrey found what she took to be a large, very sluggish, yellow grasshopper on her window sill. She caught it and showed it to a biologist friend who identified it as a locust. A search turned up thirty more equally sluggish locusts in a shrubbery near the shop. Their origin and how they came to be in Surrey in mid-winter is a total mystery.

This report of rats stealing eggs appeared in an 1865 edition of the *Zoologist*: 'The rector of a parish in Westmorland assured me he had witnessed this feat. Having lost many eggs belonging to a laying hen he was induced to watch the thief. One morning, soon after the cackling bird had given warning that she had deposited an egg, he observed two rats come out of a hole in the henhouse and proceed directly to the nest. One of the rats lay down on its side, whilst the other rat rolled the fresh egg so near it that it could embrace it with its feet. Having now obtained a secure hold of the egg, its companion dragged it into the hole by its tail and disappeared.'

In December 1983 71-year-old Dorothy Ashworth collapsed on a beach at Barton-on-Sea. All night long Smartie stayed by her side, licking her face and tugging at her coat in an effort to make her stand up. When rescuers found them the following morning, the old lady was suffering from hypothermia and died later in hospital. The amazing thing about the incident was that the six-month-old dog didn't belong to Dorothy, but to the hotel where she was staying.

# Toby

Toby was a famous train hobo of the feline world. As a young kitten he attached himself to the refreshment room at Carlisle station, soon afterwards developing a fascination with rolling stock and a wanderlust that lasted to the end of his days.

When he made his first journey nobody knows, but he soon became such a well-known commuter that London Midland Scottish gave him a tag with the message 'If found please return to Carlisle Station' to wear around his neck. Curiously enough the black cat only took north-bound trains – frequently as far as Scotland – but never ventured south of Carlisle. He had a definite preference for fish trains, although he wouldn't turn his nose up at those with a milk van either. His longest journey was 245 miles to Aberdeen and, on one occasion, he arrived at the fishing port of Stranraer, but balked at taking the steamer across to Ireland. The station master at Carlisle started a record of Toby's journeys but gave up when the cat passed the fifty-mark.

Sadly Toby's passion also cost him his life. He was strolling across the tracks at Carlisle when he was hit by a train as it came into the station.

Researchers studying six square kilometres of a jungle area flooded by the Amazon have discovered a species of fish, not yet catalogued, which flourishes in waters almost devoid of oxygen. The fish adapt to such seemingly impossible living conditions by creating a lip-like projection to the lower jaw, with which they extract oxygen from the half-millimetre gap between the water and the layer of air above it. The lip develops within hours and starts growing the moment the oxygen supply in the water drops to a dangerously low level.

# Pip

Pip was a small fox terrier bought for 7s 6d from the Battersea Dogs' Home by Cherry Kearton, a well-known big game hunter and photographer of the 1920s.

Kearton was organizing an expedition to photograph lions in their natural habitat and it wasn't long before Pip, who'd only known the streets of London, found himself in the wilds of Africa. In the days before Land Rovers and game reserves, the undertaking was both difficult and dangerous but Pip proved to be a fearless companion.

When news arrived at the camp that two man-eating lions had been spotted in the vicinity of a nearby native village, Kearton set off with Pip, his camera, eleven young Masai warriors and four Somali scouts on horseback. Eventually the lions were located and the Masai began a slow and cautious advance. Their presence whipped the big cats into a state of snarling fury. The hot air echoed with their roars and they tore at the earth with their awesome paws. The terrified Masai warriors launched repeated spear attacks but they couldn't get close enough to hit their targets. Suddenly one of the lions bounded off while the other took cover nearby. It was at this point Kearton decided to enlist the terrier's help and he urged her to find the beast for him. Pip dashed off eagerly and dived into the dried-up bed of a stream and disappeared.

A short while later the expectant silence was shattered by a terrible roar. Kearton waited but there was no other sound. Hurrying to investigate he found the lion dead with a growling Pip hanging tenaciously onto its tail. She had apparently sunk her teeth into it allowing one of the warriors to creep up and thrust his spear through the beast's heart.

Whatever we might think of killing lions, the Masai – and Kearton – were very impressed. One of the customs of their tribe is that the man who takes the lion's tail also has the honour of its mane. And the fact that the man, in this instance, was a small dog didn't change things at all. The story of Pip's triumph spread widely and earned her the nickname of 'Simba the Lion'.

In February 1989 snorkel fisherman Stephen Sheehan was killed by a giant cod off Lizard Island, Northern Queensland, Australia. He was swimming with friends when a monster potato cod head-butted him with such ferocity he lost consciousness and drowned. Potato cods can weigh as much as 250 lb and are notoriously aggressive.

# King Of Crocodiles

For ten years a giant man-eating crocodile, believed to be 140 years old, has terrorized people on the Muara Sungei Antek river, about 600 miles south east of the capital Kuala Lumpur in Malaya. The monster is easily recognizable because of his extraordinary size and very distinctive white tinge on his back and above the forelegs.

During this ten years he has killed thirteen people and all attempts to track down his lair have failed. After a savage killing in 1984 Malay witch doctors were brought in to try and charm him out into the open so he could either be shot by police sharpshooters or captured. The rituals performed were long and intensive, but they had no effect at all.

In February 1989 he struck again and claimed his thirteenth victim, a 45-year-old fisherman called Brian Tunging. The deep teeth marks scarring the side of his boat indicated Brian had literally been shaken out of his boat and into the water where the beast had then ripped him to pieces.

The 24 ft killer beast is known as Bujang Senang, meaning 'King Of Crocodiles' in the local Iban language and 'Easy-Going Bachelor' in Malay – apt because Bujang has never been seen with a mate.

To local people the King of Crocodile's great age, size, terrifying exploits and apparent invulnerability, point to something supernatural. The police, on the other hand, are simply defeated by an enemy smarter than themselves. A spokesman speaking after the latest tragedy said that, considering their past failures, police had no plans for scouring the area again.

In the late seventeenth century Shogun Tsunayoshi – known as the Dog Shogun – passed a law decreeing that all dogs in Japan must be treated kindly and addressed only in the most polite of terms. He took the law to such extremes that he ended up caring for 100,000 dogs. The result was trouble for the Exchequer, soaring inflation and the imposing of an unpopular new tax on farmers. In present day Japan the number of dogs imported has tripled over the past five years to over 7,000. A pedigree Yorkshire terrier puppy, one of the most popular breeds, costs around £335, a more exotic bitch can cost sixteen times more. Nearly 3½ million pedigree dogs are registered with the Japan Kennel Club.

In 1906 the financier Nathan Rothschild made a 'killing' on the London Stock Exchange when homing pigeons brought him news of Napoleon's defeat in the Battle of Waterloo a full day before the general public knew of it.

# Tundra

One of the American entertainment industry's rising animal stars is a six-year-old Samoyed bitch called Tundra. Tundra earns $1,000 a day and everybody agrees she deserves every cent. Talented and exceptionally bright, she can carry out more than 200 voice commands and answer more than seventy hand signals.

Her leap to stardom began after she was spotted on local TV series and signed up for the soap series, *Love Boat*. She now has a lifestyle to match her celebrity status. Her beautiful fur is groomed by a top Hollywood hairdresser, she's driven around in a studio limousine and only eats in the best restaurants. According to her proud owner, Ted Baer, the chef at one of these establishments thinks she's so clever he lets her help cook the pizza!

When in 1989 a pit bull terrier, aptly named Storm, went on a rampage in Westchester, New York State, it took a team of police paramedics to bring him under control. Storm attacked two cars and a van leaving the vehicles stranded in the street. 'Those jaws just went click and the tyres went down,' said officer Mark Califano afterwards. 'You'd have thought a butcher's knife had gone through them.' The canine vandal was tranquillized by darts fired from a safe distance of 50 yards before being netted and taken into custody.

# Chia Chia Goes To Mexico

In 1988 there were only fifteen giant pandas in the West and a dwindling world population of 900. In the light of such serious statistics London Zoo realized they couldn't allow Chia Chia, a healthy sixteen-year-old male, alone since the death of his mate in 1985, to continue as a bachelor. It was decided, therefore, to send him on a breeding mission to Mexico's national zoo in the Chapultepee Park.

Of all the zoos which had received pairs of pandas from the Chinese in the 1970s, Chapultepee Park Zoo had come out top in the breeding stakes. Four healthy cubs had been produced there, a success the Mexicans believe is due to their diet of liquidized vegetables, eggs, chicken and rice (as against a red meat 'porridge' mixture fed to them by the British, for example), and the fact they are allowed to socialize with each other more. In China pandas are considered extremely dangerous animals and the time they are allowed to spend together is limited to the four days a female is on heat. In Mexico, however, the panda couples are allowed to sniff each other through the bars and get used to each other's presence before eventually moving into the same cage.

Chia Chia arrived in Mexico to a blaze of publicity worthy of any international superstar. His welcoming party – which he attended behind a glassed-in cage – was held in a new state-of-the-art panda house and packed with all manner of dignitaries. Britain's representative, MP for Watford

Tristan Garel-Jones, gave a speech in which he said he hoped Chia Chia would 'behave like an English gentleman – but not too much!'

Chia Chia settled down immediately and seemed delighted by the proximity of Ying Ying, Liang Liang, Xiu-Hua, Shuan Shuan and Tohui, the favourite candidate for his new mate. Initially there seemed to be no romantic spark between them and when Chia met Liang Liang, a young male, they nuzzled each other so amorously through the bars that it was feared he might be gay! Fortunately when Tohui stopped playing hard to get, Chia Chia's natural instincts reasserted themselves leading everyone to hope they would soon mate and produce a family.

---

A high-tec mousetrap has recently been patented in Washington, USA. It lures the rodent into a box with the usual bait but as the creature enters, it trips a sensor that causes it to be trap-doored into a plastic bag where a pump replaces the air with carbon dioxide. In three minutes the mouse is as dead as a doornail.

---

# The Great White Killer

It was a bright February day in 1989 when Luciano Costanzo and his eighteen-year-old son, Gianluca, decided to take their boat out to sea.

Luciano was an experienced scuba diver and a mile out of the port town of Piombina, Italy, he donned his gear and jumped into the water. He'd hardly gone any distance when the massive head of a 25 ft Great White shark suddenly reared up and came straight at him. Gianluca watched in horror and disbelief as his father was dragged under by his air tank and after a few moments the churning sea began to turn red with his blood. Weeping with shock and grief, the teenager somehow managed to steer the boat back to port.

News of the tragedy spread fast and the 40,000 inhabitants of Piombino reacted with disbelief and violent rage. Officials had to step in to stop recklessly assembled posses setting out to find the killer. Swimming was also banned and the mayor forbade all boats under 18 ft long to leave port for the open sea.

The experts' attempts to trap the Great White were like scenes from the movie *Jaws*. First a diver was lowered 60 ft in a steel cage while the skipper waited above with a harpoon primed with explosives. After a while this was abandoned as too dangerous because the diver had no means of communicating with the boat. The next attempt was to pour gallons of fresh blood into the sea and wait, harpoons poised, for the monster to arrive. When this didn't work either they tried to lure it to the surface with hooks baited with cattle carcasses attached to a giant jaw-like clamp. They waited for an entire day and night – but of the Great White Killer, not a sign.

---

In November 1980 a sheepdog guarded its dead master for eleven days in the Spanish mountains. When rescuers eventually arrived on the scene they found the dog wounded, presumably from defending the corpse against wild animals. When his master's body was carried away, the dog silently vanished into the wilderness.

In 1985 the *New York Sun* reported the sad story of a captive breeding quail who died on the third day of sitting on her nest. The cock was extremely distressed. He dragged his dead mate into a corner and buried her, leaving only the long feathers of one wing exposed. This done he returned to the nest and sat on the eggs. He eventually succeeded in hatching a brood of ten young quail.

# Rebel

The twelve-week-old Alsatian puppy called Rebel that Sandra Nicholls gave her boyfriend, Roger, grew into a beautiful dog fiercely protective of them both. They adored him too but drew the line at letting him share their bedroom. Rebel didn't take kindly to this and they had to heavily barricade the door to keep him out. This perfectly natural desire for privacy, however, nearly cost them their lives.

One night in February 1989 a fire started by faulty wiring quickly spread through their Orpington house. Rebel set up a loud frantic barking and, when it failed to wake them, began hurling himself against the bedroom door until he managed to smash it open. Sandra and Roger, already well on the way to being overcome by the toxic fumes, still didn't react. Rebel dragged the bedclothes off the bed, seized Sandra by the wrist and dragged her outside into the street. Once she was safe he rushed back inside and rescued a very groggy Roger.

A spokesman for the London Fire Brigade said Rebel had saved them from certain death and that they had contacted the RSPCA to suggest he be given a bravery award. Rebel, however, was very happy with the reward he got from Sandra and Roger: kisses, cuddles – and a whole leg of roast pork.

In September 1983 eighty pilot whales were stranded by the ebbing tide on New Zealand's Tokerau Beach. Local people waded in to soothe the mammals and keep their skins wet but, when the tide came in and the refloated whales were pointed seaward, they turned around and beached themselves again. The whales were saved by a school of dolphins who came to their aid and guided them back out to sea.

Giant and lesser pandas have long been grouped together because they look so similar and their tooth and skull structures are so much alike. In 1985, however, comparisons of chromosomes, DNA structures and protein characteristics revealed that although the giant panda is a bear, the lesser panda is actually a racoon.

# 'Living Software'

A report in a 1988 issue of the American magazine *Science* revealed that more than 240 dolphins, whales and sea lions had been drafted into the US Navy in a secret programme for 'advanced biological systems'. Referred to as 'living software' and 'self-propelled marine vehicles with built-in sonar sensing system', the programme was a quiet triumph for the natural skills and intelligence of creatures who were to largely replace human divers and mechanical submersibles for recovery operations at all US Navy sea test ranges.

It all started with a Pacific white sided dolphin who was studied in 1960 to understand more about the hydrodynamics of torpedoes. This was followed by research with sea lions who were trained to respond to a sonar pinger installed in equipment to be recovered. The sea lions had to operate wearing a harness attached to a fine nylon line, swim down to depths of around 750 ft and attach a specially designed grab to the target. This system, officially called Project Quick Find, was first officially demonstrated in 1970 when the US Pacific Missile Range challenged the Navy to show them what the creatures could do. The Navy responded with a display by their champion sea lion, Turk.

Turk astounded the initially sceptical observers by hearing the pinger first time, plummeting down to the sea bed some 600 ft below, locating and fixing the recovery grab to an antisubmarine rocket all in a matter of minutes. It later took a team of four divers several hours just to check that Turk had indeed fixed the grab properly – which, of course, he had.

After this success research started with a 1,200 lb pilot whale called Morgan and a 5,500 lb killer whale called Ahah. Using a specially designed mouth-held grab of suitable proportions, these vast mammals were put through a training programme similar to that of the sea lions to recover lost torpedoes from depths of 1,654 ft. The name of this operation was Project Deep Find. After his initial training was finished, Morgan was released into the open sea. He returned voluntarily to his pen, however, and went on to have further training and became a valuable and reliable open-sea worker.

During this time dolphins were also being trained. In 1971 the US Navy employed many of them to stand guard against saboteurs in Cam Ranh Bay during the long and tragic war in Vietnam.

In 1985 the small mid-West American town of Prairie Village, Kansas, came up with a novel idea for a local TV programme. Devised by Mike Milkovich, the show used exclusively doggie actors and was aimed at an exclusively doggie audience. Mr Milkovich auditioned 150 canines to put together his cast and gave his own dog, Spot, a leading part. A doggie fashion show was a regular feature, during which Spot wore specially designed jeans, tennis shoes and a T-shirt reading: 'The only thing between me and my jeans is my fleas'. Surveys reported that the canine audience was very appreciative. They would bark and howl approval at the dogs barking and howling on the screen.

Forty-seven-year-old Bill Holmes of Codnor, Derbyshire, has let it be known he is looking for a vicar prepared to officiate at the 1989 wedding he's organizing for his pet monkeys.

In 1982 the *Weekly World News* carried the story of two-year-old Joel Zacarias, a slum child living in the outskirts of Manila, Philippines, who was saved from starvation by a mongrel dog who suckled him daily for more than a year. The case attracted a lot of attention but every time concerned people tried to intervene they were snarled off. Eventually Joel, who behaved just like a dog, was taken to a rehabilitation centre.

# Rin Tin Tin

Rin Tin Tin, adored hero of generations of children around the world, was one of a litter rescued from an abandoned dug-out in France in 1918 by an American airman called Lee Duncan.

Once back in California Rin Tin Tin, named after a little doll carried by French soldiers for luck, was trained by Lee for dog shows and he immediately showed his potential. Spotted by talent scouts he was given a part in the 1923 film *Where the North Begins*. It was a hit and a canine star was born.

Over the next nine years Rinty made more than forty movies, earned over a million dollars and kept Warner Bros solvent. A great stunt dog, Rin Tin Tin thrilled his audiences, scaling walls, running through fire and leaping off impossible heights. He was also an inspired actor when it came to portraying emotion, as can be seen in scenes where his expression was required to change from forlorn, to hopeful, to sad, to joyful in minutes.

He died in 1932 and his son, Rin Tin Tin Jr, took over starring in Westerns until 1938. Other descendants appeared in the *The Return of Rin Tin Tin* (1947) and a TV series, 'The Adventures of Rin Tin Tin', begun in 1954. The series was rerun in the 1970's and even today there are very few children who haven't heard his name.

# The First Talking Budgie

Thomas Watling was a notorious and skilful forger. In 1788 a London court found him guilty of counterfeiting banknotes and he was sent to a penal colony in New South Wales. The life he found waiting for him there wasn't bad at all. His 'artistic talents' were quickly recognized, earning him the envied position of assistant to the colony physician, Dr James White.

Watling was fascinated by Australia's exotic and abundant wildlife and his privileged position gave him time to study it. It wasn't long before he discovered that the pretty, brightly-coloured birds he saw everywhere were very friendly and could be taught to speak. He tamed one and spent hours training it.

One day Dr White came looking for him in his hut. He stared around the empty room and was just about to leave again when a voice suddenly piped, 'How do you do, Dr White?' The man was totally astonished when he later discovered it was actually a bird who'd spoken. That little bird was the first talking budgerigar on record.

Thomas Watling was later pardoned by the first Governor of New South Wales, but freedom didn't lessen his passion for budgies. He continued to tame them and teach them to speak until his death.

The komondor, a huge dog with a shaggy, white corded coat native to Hungary, is being employed by sheep farmers in the United States because of its success in dealing with coyotes, notorious for decimating flocks. The komondor stands at 2 ft, weighs approximately 100 lb, has fierce territorial instincts and is impressively powerful and fast on its feet. Since 1972, when the government banned the use of poison because of its effect on other wildlife, the komondor has been the farmers' main defence against the coyotes.

# Bootsie

One day a little grey and white mongrel appeared on a platform at Charing Cross Station guarding a pair of men's shoes. He was such a strange sight that many of the rush hour commuters paused to say a few words and try and pat him on the head. But the animal took his responsibility very seriously and, like any good guard dog, saw them all off with a menacing snarl. The little dog sat on the platform all day long but the owner of the shoes – who was presumably his master too – never turned up.

As he would let no one near him, a policeman was eventually called to deal with the situation. After a lot of coaxing (and the help of a noose at the end of a pole), the officer succeeded in scooping up both dog and shoes and delivering them to the Battersea Dogs' home.

Even there the dog, now named Bootsie, refused to be separated from his master's shoes. The *Daily Mirror* published a picture of him carrying them in his mouth with the result that 700 people wrote in to offer him a home. Bootsie and shoes eventually went to a lady in Bristol who travelled down to London especially to get him. He quickly settled in, discarded the shoes and lived happily ever after.

# England's Saviour

On 1 May 1989 the Tower of London celebrated a great historic event. The first raven to be born in captivity at the Tower for more than three hundred years was hatched in the shadow of the White Tower. No cannons were fired in salute, no firework display was organized, but eager press photographers and reporters jostled to record the chick's public debut 43 days later. The wonderbird was a great success. Although its legs were bandaged to strengthen a weakness, it displayed a ravenous appetite pecking furiously at chunks of raw meat.

The Tower of London, built soon after 1066 and now custodian of the crown jewels, has always had a raven population and legend warns that the kingdom will fall should they ever leave. It is said that there were so many of them during the reign of Charles II that he decided to get rid of them. His wise advisors persuaded him to keep a few, but nevertheless the legend of the destruction of the empire is believed to date from that period.

Charlie and Rhys, the chick's parents, who were brought to the Tower as fledglings from the wild, were justifiably proud of their achievement. So were the Tower staff who had kept an anxious guarded eye on the whole process. As Yeoman Ravenmaster John Wilmington said, 'Royalty, the fortress and England are now safe'.

> To cure himself of convulsions, a young peasant from Jinlin province in north-eastern China, ate more than 1,800 live poisonous snakes over a two year period. The cure was effective but Wang Biao became so addicted to snakes he needed to swallow one before every meal.

It has long puzzled animal researchers how male elephants are able to track down a female on heat even if she is many miles away. Or how random groups of elephants, also separated by miles, somehow manage to meet up at the same place. Then in 1985 Katherine Payne, of Cornell University, New York State, became aware of a spasmodic throbbing in the air that coincided with a fluttering on an elephant's forehead in the group she was studying. Further research with sophisticated ultrasonic recording equipment revealed that elephants communicate by using sounds at such a low frequency the human ear is incapable of detecting them.

# Lady

Lady was a celebrated telepathic horse from Richmond in Virginia, USA, who regularly performed to admiring audiences for almost thirty years. She communicated by indicating with her muzzle letters on an enormous, specially designed display board. She allegedly gave advice on personal problems, predicted Harry Truman's victory in the presidential elections of 1948 and helped police in the sad case of a missing child. When asked about his whereabouts, Lady responded immediately spelling out: 'Pittsfield water wheel'. This cryptic answer meant nothing until an inspired police captain suggested the horse might mean: 'Field and Wilde Water Pitt', the name of a nearby quarry. A search was promptly undertaken and the boy's body was found where she said it would be.

In 1927 the parapsychologists J B and Louisa Rhine pitched a tent near the horse's famous red stable. They wanted to investigate their theory that Lady was receiving the answers to questions put to her telepathically from her owner. To their disappointment, however, they were unable to prove this conclusively.

# Lucy

Lucy is a six-year-old cocker spaniel who brought the house down at the 1985 Cruft's Dog Show when she demonstrated how she answers the telephone.

But Lucy's no performing dog, she has been specially trained to be the 'ears' of a deaf person. She reacts to the sound of an alarm clock, a doorbell, the ping of a microwave oven and the sound of a smoke alarm. When the telephone rings, she picks up the receiver to attract the attention of the deaf person she's assigned to. People who may not be able to hear a telephone ringing, for example, can often hear the voice at the other end with the aid of a special volume control.

Lucy was trained by a charity called Hearing Dogs for the Deaf which was founded in 1982 by deaf actress Elizabeth Quinn, star of *Children of a Lesser God*.

The humpback whale creates the longest and most complex repertoire of sounds of any known animal. Not only do their sounds vary from year to year, they also 'speak' with regional differences.

Rats can squeeze through a hole the size of a 50p coin, climb practically any vertical surface, tread water for up to three days, jump three feet, drop safely from a height of 45 ft, kill quarry more than twice their own size and chew through live electrical cable. In 1348 they brought the Black Death to Europe, a plague which killed 25 million people, and today are responsible for the spread of diseases such as typhus, trichinosis, Lassa fever and salmonella. In the United States they gnaw through more than $1 billion worth of property a year. One pair of breeding rats can have as many as 15,000 descendants in a single year.

# Balto

When in January 1925 a diptheria outbreak started in Nome, Alaska, the city made the alarming discovery that their supply of antitoxin was insufficient to stave off an epidemic. Appalling weather conditions made flying out of the question, so it was decided to use relay teams of sled dogs to rush the serum from Nemana 600 miles away.

Gunnar Kasson's team was lead by a black, long-haired malamute called Balto. This extraordinary and valiant dog led his team through the rough interior of Alaska and across the frozen Bering Sea, struggling through blizzards, buffeted by 80 mph winds at temperatures down to $-50°F$, often unable to see but always managing to scent his trail. He trekked across huge snow drifts that toppled the sled, iced-over lagoons and vast tracts of splintered ice shards that cut the dogs' feet like glass. Conditions were so bad and visibility so reduced that for much of the journey Kasson had to rely totally on the skill of his lead dog. Balto's team was the first to enter stricken Nome on 2 February at exactly 5.36 am. A statue of Balto stands in Central Park, New York, commemorating the Nome Serum Run. The inscription reads:

'Dedicated to the indomitable spirit of the sled dogs that relayed antitoxin 600 miles over rough ice, treacherous waters, through arctic blizzards from Nemana to the relief of stricken Nome in the winter of 1925. Endurance, Fidelity, Intelligence.'

# The High Fliers

Pigeon racing is a sport enjoyed by more than 75,000 registered owners, of every profession and social class. Actor Yul Brynner was a pigeon fancier, as is retired union boss Lord Chappie, boxer Marvin Hagler, the King of Thailand, Coronation Street's Jack Duckworth and, of course, the Queen, who has a loft near Sandringham. The racing season lasts from April to September and the National Racing Pigeon Show – the pigeon world's equivalent to Cruft's – gets all the enthusiasts in a flap.

The sport evolved from the ancient practice of sending messages by pigeon, something that has been done since Biblical times. Pigeon racing is Belgium's national sport and it took hold in Great Britain in about 1871.

Most pigeons cost between £20 and £25 but Michael Massarella, of Europe's biggest pedigree racing pigeon stud near Loughborough, Leicestershire, paid a record £77,000 for a Dutch-bred bird called Emerald. He didn't have to wait long for a return on his investment, though. A fancier paid £2,400 for Emerald's first offspring – before the egg had even hatched!

The birds fly at speeds up to 70 mph and can cover 700 miles a day. No one really knows quite how they find their way home but the accepted theory is that they use a combination of light, smell and the Earth's natural magnetic field to navigate. The racing pigeon's renowned sense of direction isn't infallible, though. When, in the summer of 1988, a bird got lost on its way to Berkshire from France, it had to be flown home in an aeroplane.

---

The venom of the Russell's viper aids the clotting process and is used to stop bleeding in haemophiliacs. The venom of the deadly Malayan pit viper, however, has the opposite effect. Research is now focused on its ability to dissolve blood clots that can cause coronary thrombosis and some kinds of strokes.

---

# Courtaud

One of the most notorious villains in animal history was a French wolf called Courtaud. He was the leader of a large pack of outlaw wolves who attacked the flocks driven outside the walls of Paris to graze in the surrounding countryside.

The pack first made their appearance during the summer of 1447 and for three years menaced the entire area. Their reign of terror culminated one bloody February day in 1450 when they reputedly entered the city through a breach in the wall and massacred forty people.

Shockwaves of outrage and fear swept through Paris. Armed posses of frenzied citizens were organized to hunt out the fiends' lairs, but repeatedly failed to find them. In desperation it was decided to lay a trail of fresh meat and lure them into the square in front of Notre Dame. The ploy worked. The slavering wolves arrived to find a waiting mob who set about them with staves, knives and anything else they could lay their hands on. Courtaud and every last one of his murderous gang were killed.

Recent research is suggesting that pigeons may be as intelligent as chimpanzees and dolphins. A group of ravens in Oregon began picking up stones and bombarding people who strayed too close to their nests. In Texas, green jays have been seen selecting twigs to poke under loose bark to dislodge insects. Sea otters open shells by pounding them with stones. Scientific research is uncovering new proof of animals' intelligence all the time. Professor Donald R Griffin of Rockerfeller University, New York, and one of the leading authorities on animal intelligence, believes evidence indicates that animals are capable of what he calls 'conscious mental experience'.

# Tyke

In February 1980, three-year-old Michael Surman decided his dog Tyke was hungry. He dragged a stool over to the stove, clambered up and set about making his pet some breakfast. But while he was trying to light the gas, his pyjamas caught fire and seconds later he was staggering around screaming with agony.

The cross-bred collie leapt into action. He knocked the toddler to the floor and rolled over him to smother the flames with his body. Tyke's prompt intervention saved Michael's life but, sadly, couldn't prevent him from being badly burned.

> In September 1988 a four-year-old Alsatian, Rocky, was stabbed three times in the head and body when he saved his handler from the attack of a vicious knifeman. PC Lehec went to make an arrest while on temporary duty in Brixton. Rocky received a bravery award, an engraved plaque, from the Blue Cross Animal Hospital.

# Kanzi

Kanzi, a pygmy chimpanzee whose achievements have received a lot of media attention, is a star pupil of the American Language Research Centre.

Like the Centre's other chimps, Kanzi has been taught to communicate by punching out geometrical symbols on a keyboard. Where he has outstripped them, however, is in his unique ability to understand spoken English without accompanying gestures. Some of the requests put to him are complex. Like, for example, 'Will you get a nappy for your sister Mulika?' The other chimps, although able to respond well enough to commands given on the keyboard, are confused when asked orally. Kanzi, on the other hand, does equally well either way.

He is also able to identify objects by name, comment on an activity he will be doing in the future and describe actions he wants to carry out. Although he can't construct grammatical sentences, he will often make two or three word statements without any prompting. He also makes spontaneous demands of his own. He will ask to play a particular game, for example, or ask to be taken to the tree house in the Centre's 55 acres of wooded grounds.

One of his best friends was a chimp called Austin and the two were in the habit of having a romp together every evening before bedtime. When Austin was moved away, Kanzi missed him a lot. He sat down at the keyboard and typed out the symbols for 'Austin' and 'TV'. The director of research on ape language, Dr Sue Savage-Rumbaugh, understood immediately that he was referring to a video of Austin he'd seen several times before. She brought it to him to watch, after which he settled down happily.

A bad tempered hippopotamus rammed and overturned a canoe on Zambia's Kafue River in 1986. Eight unfortunate people died.

In 1987 Mrs Hudson of Hants split up with her live-in lover. They had no problem dividing up the china, linen and record collection, but could not agree on who should take Chocolate Drop, the cat. She was eventually 'catnapped' by Ken James, who refused to give her back. The question was finally resolved by the Bournemouth County Court. Mr James contested that as he'd found the cat wandering as a stray in 1985, she was rightfully his. Mrs Hudson insisted she'd registered Chocolate Drop with the Burmese Cat Club in her name. The judge ruled in Mrs Hudson's favour and ordered that Chocolate Drop be returned home.

> The owl can locate the position of a sound better than any other creature. Its brain creates a sound map that pinpoints the exact location of the last sound it heard.

# Storsjoodjuret

Storsjoodjuret is Sweden's famous monster of Lake Storsjon, reputed to be a huge serpentine creature measuring between 10 and 20 metres in length. One of the most recent sightings occurred on 10 July 1985 when a family of three spotted the coal-black monster undulating through the deep waters with its humps clearly visible above the surface.

Swedish authorities take the existence of Storsjoodjuret very seriously. The country administration of Jamtland has made a legal precedent by declaring that anyone trying to capture or kill the creature can now be prosecuted under section 14 of the Nature Conservation act.

> More than 10,000 cats are 'employed' by the British Government to keep official buildings free from rodents.

# Cho-Lee and The Pigs

Cho-Lee was born on a small farm near Canton in China. She had three brothers and a twin sister but the only creatures with whom she felt an affinity were the pigs the family kept in the back yard. From the moment she was old enough to toddle her parents couldn't keep her out of the sty and – by the time she was three and had moved in with them – they stopped trying. The pigs accepted her from the beginning as one of their own and Cho-Lee lived exclusively on sow's milk until she was five. After that she gobbled swill at the trough with the rest of them.

Her parents were extremely embarrassed by the situation and tried to keep it a carefully guarded secret. But, inevitably, word got out and on at least two occasions outraged villagers stormed the farm to rescue her. Each time, however, the same thing happened. Cho-Lee shrank away from her would-be rescuers while the pigs, squealing and grunting with rage, formed a protective circle around her. The animals were punched, kicked and beaten with sticks but they continued to stand their ground and refused to let anyone near. Totally bewildered, the villagers eventually gave up and went away.

When it became known that Cho-Lee was living with the pigs from choice, an animal behaviourist from Peking arrived to study the case. Dr Chou Lai-Myung found her of normal intelligence and in excellent health. But after observing her for several days, all he could say was that for some incomprehensible reason she thought, felt and acted just like a pig.

---

In Greek myth the chimera is a fire-breathing monster with the head of a lion, the body of a goat, and the tail of a serpent. Today science creates weird hybrid creatures for research purposes. One such example is the Sheep-Goat chimera. Its creation is a complex process: one embryo is taken from a pregnant sheep, another from a pregnant goat. Then cells from both embryos are combined to form a sheep-goat embryo. This embryo is then returned to the sheep or goat host womb where it continues normal gestation until birth. It is thought that enabling one animal to give birth to an animal of a different species could save endangered animals from extinction in the future.

In 1963 a US athlete broke a world record when he was timed at 27 mph during a 100 yard sprint. A cheetah, however, can average 56 mph with short bursts of more than 60 mph.

The RSPCA was founded by Rev Arthur Broome and Richard Martin, together with other humanitarians in 1824. It is the oldest animal protection society in the world and, at a time when brutality to animals was the rule of the day, its establishment was a cause for ridicule and scorn. Its status changed, becoming acceptable to society when the then Princess Victoria became its patron at the age of fifteen.

Bats navigate in darkness by sending out a supersonic note which comes back as an echo and gives it time to avoid any obstacles. When a baby bat is born the mother hangs upside down and uses her tail and wings as a cradle. The baby then climbs on to its mother and holds tight with its specially hooked baby teeth. The temperature of a bat's body can vary by as much as 50°F and they spend five-sixths of their lives hanging upside down. In many countries bats are associated with evil and death, but in China they are considered lucky and are a symbol of health and happiness.

When the ancient citadel of Corinth was subjected to a surpise attack late one night it found all the soldiers sleeping. It was left to the fifty courageous watchdogs to defend the town. A ferocious and valiant attempt was made by the animals to keep the invaders at bay but, despite their brave fight, all but one were killed. This lone survivor raced to the gates of the town and sounded the alarm which finally woke the sleeping soldiers. They rushed to their posts and eventually the attack was repulsed. The hero of that night was given a pension and a solid silver collar bearing the inscription: 'To Soter, defender and saviour of Corinth, placed under the protection of his friends.'

# Baby

Forty-four-year-old secretary Bonita Whitfield was puzzled (and more than a little put out!) when her mongrel, Baby, started persistently sniffing the back of one of her legs. The collie-Dobermann cross-breed did it so frequently that Bonita finally investigated the spot, discovering a strange lump that she took to be a mole. She was not particularly worried, however, and soon put it out of her mind. Then, one warm day in May 1989, she was in the garden wearing a pair of shorts when Baby not only sniffed the lump – she actually tried to bite it off! 'Almost,' Bonita said afterwards, 'as if she knew it shouldn't be there.'

It was then Bonita became sufficiently concerned to mention it to a colleague, a former nurse who advised her to see a doctor immediately. Bonita made the appointment that was to save her life. Her doctor sent her straight from the surgery to King's College Hospital where the lump was diagnosed as a cancerous tumour and removed the same day.

Dr Hywel Williams, who performed the operation, was extremely impressed by Baby's obvious awareness that the mole on her owner's leg was potentially fatal, speculating that the dog had actually been able to 'smell' the cancer developing. Dr Williams now intends to start a research programme, working with Baby to find out if she is able to 'sniff out' cancerous growths in other patients as well.

> For years scientists had been puzzling over the tiny sand-bubbler crab of Australia. Although it has no lungs, it spends long periods out of water and they wanted to know how it breathed. Then in the mid 1980s Australian scientist David P Maitland discovered that membranes on their legs let in air while keeping water and sand out. He concluded that the membranes, which had previously been thought to be ears, were really a sort of lung.

Sampson, an eighteen-month-old golden retriever, survived on a cliff ledge for a fortnight by licking rainwater off his coat. Sampson, who broke both front legs when he fell 50 ft down a cliff at Budleigh Salterton, Devon, was eventually rescued when he was spotted by a walker on the beach.

# Rocky Of Naples

Penninata a San Gennaro dei Poveri (aptly meaning St Gennaro's Hill of the Poor) is one of the most wretched streets in the whole of Naples. In one of the Penninata's crumbling tenements a family composed of two women, whose husbands had been murdered by the Neapolitan Mafia, lived with their ten children in a single room. But despite the horrendous over-crowding, they still took in a stray three-year-old Alsatian to keep as a pet. Although it meant finding the extra lire to feed him, Rocky was a welcome addition to the family. He was a gentle patient dog always ready to play with the children who had no proper toys. His true worth, however, was only revealed by a tragedy.

On a spring afternoon in 1986 23-year-old Giuseppina was alone in the room with two of her daughters, Emilia aged three and Patrizia aged six. Realizing she needed something from the shops, she decided to pop out and leave the children with the dog. Seconds after she left a faulty Calor gas cylinder, that provided their only heating, started to leak and a fire started.

Rocky's response was immediate. Barking furiously he bounded over to the bed where Emilia was sleeping, seized hold of her dress and dragged her screaming into the narrow street. Meanwhile Giuseppina had returned to find flames leaping out of the window and a crowd of horrified neighbours looking on. The general cry of joy and relief that went up when Rocky emerged with Emilia was short-lived, however, when Giuseppina realized Patrizia was still inside. The blaze was fast getting out of control and as the distraught woman rushed towards the building she was seized by neighbours and forcibly held back. But Rocky didn't hesitate. He plunged back into the inferno and a moment later Patrizia stumbled out into her mother's arms.

During all this the fire brigade were manoeuvring their cumbersome equipment up the hundred or so steps to the burning tenement. When they finally arrived and fought their way inside, they found Rocky sprawled half-way across the room. He'd been choked by toxic fumes and part of his coat was on fire. Giuseppina and her children buried the brave animal in a small patch of earth nearby. Local people placed flowers and cards on his pauper's grave and wept unashamedly. Misery, deprivation and violence was the everyday reality of their slum community and they'd come to expect little else. But Rocky, who'd given freely of love, courage and the priceless treasure of life itself, had reminded them that good does exist and had touched their hearts forever.

In January 1980 an old ape called Meg astounded keepers at Chester Zoo by giving birth to Gemma, her fifteenth youngster at the respectable age of thirty-two. That is the same as a woman having a baby at sixty-five.

In November 1975 an inspector stopped a London bound Swiss lorry on the A2 between Dover and Dartford and found a 3 ft ape sitting next to the driver. The fact that he was Fernand Montendon's valued friend and travelling companion didn't cut any ice. Monsieur Montendon was fined £200 by Dover magistrates for breaking anti-rabies regulations.

A report in the *Niagara Falls Gazette* of Ontario in August 1924 tells of a fiendish eagle with a wingspan of 8 ft who lifted a fourteen-year-old boy weighing 97 lb and carried him 5 ft before his clothing gave way. The boy hung onto the bird and managed to force it against a wire fence of the golf course where the incident took place. A man rushed to his aid and killed the bird.

# Coco The Duck

Coco, French for 'darling' or 'sweetie pie', was a very contented duck who made his home on the River Vézère that runs past the small town of Montignac in the Dordogne, France. He liked his reedy habitat. There were fish aplenty, weeds to nibble and other ducks for company. Naturally friendly and outgoing Coco was soon so tame townspeople often met him waddling aimiably around their streets. People stopped to say 'bonjour' and children gave him pieces of bread and eventually his name. But the town's hunters, most of whom belonged to France's newly-formed Hunters' Party, were not at all pleased with Coco's popularity. They prided themselves on the pedigree ducks they raised for sport along the river banks and, not being a pure-bred specimen, they feared Coco would contaminate their colony with his proletarian blood-lines. They called a top-level meeting where, in his absence and without representation, Coco was accused and found guilty of rape, harassment and infanticide. This last indictment came about when one of the hunters claimed he had seen Coco attacking eggs and killing ducklings. Maurice Debord, the local water bailiff, was elected executioner. At dawn the next day the fearless man went down to the quayside where Coco was known to waddle around looking for breakfast and he blasted him with his shotgun.

The news of the duck's death caused an uproar. Children wept and Coco's sorrowful friends filed a private prosecution against the hunters. They also dug up a law prohibiting the discharge of firearms within 150 metres of occupied houses. The Hunter's Party, which was preparing for its first-ever campaign in the European elections, said they didn't know whether Coco's killers were their members or not but that they hoped one dead duck wouldn't lose them any votes.

But to his admirers Coco was very much more than just a dead duck. One of them, a member of the Green Party, made a statement in which he described Coco as 'a martyr who will hopefully go not only to a better place but leave a better one behind'.

> In 1983 miners at Britain's largest undersea pit at Ellington Colliery, Northumberland, discovered a robin 600 ft underground and five miles from the shaft bottom. The bird was alive but in a deep torpor and could have been lying there for a very long time. Brought back up to the surface, it soon recovered and was released unharmed.

# Bosco – Mayor of Sunol

In 1981 twelve men sitting around a bar in Sunol, California, lamented the lack of elected officials in their town. Two of the men present were eager to stand for mayor but another patron nominated Bosco, a creature of impeccable character well-liked by all. There was a show of hands and Bosco won. In 1989 the 85 lb part black Labrador, part Rottweiler had been efficiently carrying out his duties as mayor for eight years. Every Halloween, cheered by Sunol's 1,500 inhabitants, he heads the town parade, wearing a red satin bow around his neck. His popularity has grown with each passing year and when another dog recently ran against him, his support was so strong the election had to be cancelled.

In 1987, however, the cares of office became a little too irksome for the high-minded dog and he took himself off on an unscheduled holiday. His disappearance was a cause of great concern and the whole town turned out to look for him. Posters were put up all over Alameda County, local media spread the news and the surrounding woods were subjected to a thorough search. When Bosco strolled back into town six days later the people of Sunol heaved a collective sigh of relief and welcomed their mayor with a slap-up steak and gravy dinner.

> When Towser the cat died in 1987, one month before her 24th birthday, the world lost one of the greatest mousers of all times. Her territory was the Glenturret distillery near Crieff, Tayside, where it is said she accounted for a staggering 28,899 mice. During her long and distinguished life Towser became a TV personality and friend of royalty – a taped cassette of her exploits was given to Prince William and Prince Harry. Towser is buried in the hills above Glenturret.

# Batir

On 13 July 1983 Tass released an extraordinary account of a thirteen-year-old talking elephant called Batir. The animal was first discovered chatting to himself late one night six years earlier by his keeper, who reported the astonishing occurrence to his superiors.

Initial scepticism turned to excitement when Soviet zoologists moved in to study the case, and made recordings of Batir's twenty or so phrases, which included 'Batir is good' and 'Have you watered the elephant?'

The Young Communist League paper *Komsomolskay Pravda*, ran an article claiming that the elephant had merely learnt to repeat the admiring comments of zoo visitors in order to get a few extra titbits of food. Another source, however, claimed that Batir, who had never mixed with other elephants, was not simply parroting, but actually using speech with rational intent.

Five seals were used in the main role of *Seal Morning*, a TV drama in six episodes based on the autobiographical story of an orphan girl in the 1930s who finds a baby seal abandoned on a beach. Like the orphan of the book, all the seals had been washed up on beaches as babies.

Skinnybone is one of Don Crown's troupe of performing dogs that tour the Northern club circuit. Skinnybone is a hugely talented dancer and his star turn is an amazing acrobatic break-dancing routine.

In Britain 6.4 million people keep a dog as a pet; 6.2 million keep a cat and 1.8 million keep a budgie.

It was a rather bizzare pigeon hunt that took place in 1977 at Horsholm, thirty miles north of Copenhagan in Denmark. No game was bagged that day but one of the three intrepid hunters was seriously injured when he was shot – by a dog! The incident happened when the hunters laid their shotguns on the ground to discuss their disappointing results. One of the dogs ambled over, accidentally treading on the trigger of a shotgun and loosing off both barrels. The 52-year-old man was hit in the legs; the dog suffered a broken claw.

# Bibliography

*Psychic Animals* by Dennis Bardens (London, Hale, 1987)

*Intelligent and Loyal: A Celebration of the Mongrel* by Jilly Cooper (London, Methuen, 1989)

*The Story of the Battersea Dogs' Home* by Gloria Cottesloe (Newton Abbot, David & Charles, 1979)

*The Secret Power of Cats* by David Greene (London, Methuen, 1984)

*The Story of Greyfriars Bobby* by Forbes McGregor (Edinburgh, Ampersand, 1986)

*Working Dogs* by Joan Palmer (Wellingborough, Patrick Stephens, 1983)

*The Animals Who's Who* by Ruthven Tremain (London, Routledge & Kegan Paul, 1982)

*The Guinness Book of Pet Records* by Gerald Wood (London, Guinness Superlatives, 1984)